The
Mystery Fancier

Wildside Press / 301-762-1305

L6010309

Title Information:

978-1-4344-3632-0

The Mystery
Fancier, Vol. 6,
No. 4

Volume 6, Number 4
July/August 1982

The Mystery Fancier

Volume 6, Number 4
July/August 1982

TABLE OF CONTENTS

The Mystery Fancier
(USPS:428-590)
is edited and published bi-monthly by
Guy M. Townsend
1711 Clifty Drive
Madison, IN 47250

SUBSCRIPTION RATES: Domestic second class mail, $12.00 per year (6 is-
sues); overseas surface mail, $12.00; overseas airmail, $18.00. Overseas subscribers please pay in international money order, check drawn
on U.S. bank, or currency; no checks drawn on foreign banks, please.
Single copy price: $2.50

Second class postage paid at Madison, Indiana.

WILDSIDE PRESS

Mysteriously Speaking . . .

Profuse apologies to all for both the poor quality of printing in and the lateness of 6:3. The two were related. It's a long story, as most of mine are, but I'll have to cut it short since this issue is already bursting at the seams even without my ramblings. Here goes. TMF 5:6 through 6:2 were printed at a shop outside of Boston, because the cost of printing anything in this part of Indiana is outrageous. Those Massachusetts boys did a pretty good job, but they hit me with two price increases between 6:1 and 6:2, so I had to start thinking again about how I could cut costs. Then, one fateful night, as the cold north wind whispered menacingly through the broken, leaning gravestones which clutter the neglected cemetery which is all that stands between my dark and brooding ancestral pile (built from the ill-gotten gains of my great-great-grandfather, Talbot Townsend, who made a mint by selling books on ethics to politicians great and small throughout this land; the books, which were actually only blocks of wood with covers attached, looked great on bookshelves, and, though old Talbot never pointed out to the politicians that the "books" couldn't actually be read, he never had a complaint from a dissatisfied customer) and the awful Madison Moor (of infamous memory), a lonely thought found its way into my fevered brain, which was still suffering from the after effects of a dreaded but little known disease which I had contracted while engaged upon a mission which.... But I was going to cut this short, wasn't I? Well, I decided to print TMF myself. To that end I purchased various pieces of equipment and built myself a little shop (at one end of a larger storage building) in which to house my printing operation. Only the equipment wasn't delivered until many weeks after the agreed-upon time, and when it was delivered it didn't work. Several efforts at repairing it were made by a supposedly qualified individual--with long intervals of time in between, of course--and when one piece of equipment (a Multilith 1250 offset press) was finally in running condition (more or less), I discovered that the paper plate maker I had purchased simply wouldn't do the job even if it were in running condition (which it wasn't). Cutting out the painful details, I got rid of the plate maker, acquired a graphics camera in its place, converted the printing shop into a part-time darkroom, latched on to a metal plate burner, and several months later--and thousands of dollars lighter--I was ready to go. Only I wasn't exactly sure how to operate all that machinery.... So, that's why 6:3 wasn't quite beautiful. I hope to improve with practice, and this issue will show how well (or poorly) my improvement is coming along.

By the way, 6:4 will be followed very shortly by 6:5, as most of 6:5 will be made up of an astonishingly complete index to the first five volumes of TMF which Charlie Cook has just completed. Charlie spent countless hours poring over the first thirty-one issues of TMF and compiling an index which should run to about forty of these pages. He has even provided me with camera-ready copy, thus eliminating the need for me to put my already questionable sanity to the inhuman stress and strain of having to type up yet another LIST! The balance of 6:5 will be made up of reviews, abbreviated installments of Verdicts and Steve's Mystery*File. I hope that you will all agree with me that Charlie's index is a tool of the greatest utility and value. A pleasant side effect of devoting most of 6:5 to the index is that it should enable me to get this magazine back on schedule at last--before, I dearly hope, the postal service decides to jerk my second-class mailing permit for falling so far behind.

The latest issue of Andy Jaysnovitch's *Not So Private Eye* arrived long before I got out 6:3, so Andy's letter on the back page of the last TMF didn't do anything to increase advance sales of TNSPE. But let me tell you, folks, TNSPE is a beaut, and if you don't have it you ought to. It is beautifully printed, for one thing, with a wrap-around cover by Tom Fisher and interior artwork by Tom Fisher and Brad Foster, both of whom are masters of their craft. Then there's the article about reptiles in the sewers by Bill Crider (who is a dead ringer for Adolphe Menjou).... That's Andy Jaysnovitch, 6 Dana Estates Dr., Parlin, NJ 08859; send him two bucks and a copy of this delightful magazine will be on its way to you via first class mail.

On the subject of delightful magazines, another one that you shouldn't miss is Jeff Meyerson's *Poisoned Pen*. After four years of printing in mimeo, Jeff has, with 5:1, gone to offset printing, and the result is easier to read and more pleasing to the eye. Also with 5:1, Jeff has switched from a bi-monthly to a quarterly schedule. At the same time, he has increased the size of each issue, so that the total page count remains about the same. Many TMFers already subscribe to *Pen*, but for those who don't (yet) I might say that it is somewhat more fannish (using that word in the non-pejorative sense) than TMF, and the average *Pen* contains more articles than the average TMF, although those articles are, of necessity, shorter than those in TMF. The address is Jeff Meyerson, 50 First Place, Brooklyn, NY 11231, and the subscription rates are: $10 domestic third class; $12 domestic first class; $10 overseas surface rate; and $24 overseas airmail. Single issues are $3.00.

And there's one more publication I'd like to alert you to while I'm at it. *Echoes*, published and edited by Tom and Ginger Johnson respectively, is a bi-monthly magazine for pulp fans. The Johnsons started *Echoes* with a "Special Issue" dated June 1982 with articles by Bob Sampson, Nick Carr, Link Hullar, and Ginger Johnson, including biographical essays on seven of today's leading pulp fans. This issue was graced, as was the

(Continued on page 39)

The Tod Hunter Question
By David E. Funct

For every Carroll John Daly and Frederick Nebel, pulp writers who are at least remembered, there were a hundred like Tod Hunter, who is not. Hunter was one of those back-of-the-book guys seemingly there just to fill space between the name writers and the beginning of the hair and frog raising ads. From the looks of things, he never really established himself anywhere, never got a good series going, probably never got his name on the cover.

I might not have noticed him myself if he hadn't turned up in the same magazine with W.T. (Todhunter) Ballard. This seemed a rather large coincidence, so I put myself on the lookout. So far I've unearthed more than a dozen stories in a surprising variety of pulps. Two more of these appeared along with Ballard stories, but the rest were on their own.

Three out of thirteen is suspicious but hardly conclusive. In any case, thirteen in my small collection means there are probably many more. It should be safe to say Tod Hunter was a very prolific fellow.

Busy with other writers the last few months, I haven't given Tod much thought. But just three weeks ago a new piece of evidence arrived on my doorstep, and things started clicking. Now I don't know if I have solved a mystery or deepened it.

†

The earliest Hunter story I've found is "Cupid's Last Stand," in *Argosy All-Story* for October 13, 1923. "Cupid aimed his arrow at Joe Two Trees," says the blurb, "but Joe aimed back." Navajo Joe, a confirmed woman-hater, nearly succumbs to a maiden named Shawnee Belle. The third-person storytelling is nothing special, but some of the dialogue is as funny as you could want.

Another from the same magazine, of February 2, 1924, is "Warp and Woof." Two college football stars with crazy nicknames are great buddies until a flirty cheerleader somes between them.

TOD HUNTER

3

The love stuff gets a bit soppy here, but again the humor pulls it through.

The next one turns up in the second July 1926 issue of *Clues*. This is when the title still belonged to Clayton Magazines, publishers of *Ace-High* and *Ranch Romances*. The story here, "Mr. Brilliance," is about a professional know-it-all travelling with a carnival. His omniscience is put to the test when his friend the clown is killed.

Hunter apparently worked all the major chains. He appeared in Street & Smith's *Detective Story* in January 1928 with "Dance of Death." In this one a former ballet star tries to murder his unfaithful wife with a dance he learned in Haiti.

Flynn's Detective Fiction is represented by "Three Killers," from January 19, 1929. Police Lieutenant Marvin Kane comes to the conclusion that all three suspects in the case are guilty. More interesting than the earlier tales because Kane narrates. Not as sharp as the Continental Op, but he dishes out plenty of wit.

DANCE OF DEATH
By TOD HUNTER

The only series character to surface is attorney Aaron Egmont, who appears in two issues of *Detective Fiction Weekly*. In "The Holdup Suit," of April 8, 1930, Egmont's flashily dressed client is an easy target for a robbery frame. In "The Craven Club," a considerably better story from August 22, 1930, he attends a fraternity reunion. After a brother with a grudge enters shooting, Egmont is hard-put to prove him innocent of three murders.

✝

The most unusual Hunter story has got to be "The Iron Heel," from the September 1931 *Strange Tales*. In this one a modern Achilles finds bullets can't hurt him except you-know-where. A specially-made shoe helps him pull several robberies but eventually prove his undoing.

Hunter's only appearance in *Black Mask* came in September 1933, an issue which also contained a Bill Lennox story by Ballard. Hunter is nearly lost among all the big guns: Whitfield, Torrey, Gardner, and Nebel. The nine-page story, "Wolf Trap," concerns the hunt for an over-weight gang boss called The Wolf. First person narration by an undercover cop named Trask makes this one of Hunter's better hardboiled efforts.

I was more than a little surprised to find Hunter in *Spicy Detective*, but, true to form, it is above average work. "Death Rides Bareback," from December 1934, features Dave Evans, a racetrack playboy who has never lost a bet. When the impossible happens--he loses--he knows it's dirty tricks and plays detec-

tive to get his luck back on track. Evans encounters and con-
quers the obligatory bimbos along the way, but he handles them
with a bit more class than his peer Dan Turner.

Another *Spicy Detective* story, from March, 1936, was an
even bigger surprise. The hero of "The Titmouse Affair" is the
eccentric consulting detective Sherlike Tarts. With the aid of
his ever-ready companion and narrator, Irene Watabod, Tart
tracks a vicious slasher who believes himself a bird. Despite
the wacky plot, this parody is really quite well done and de-
serves to be reprinted if it hasn't been already.

WOLF TRAP

Hunter also made it into the Tro-
jan line's less spicy entry, *Private
Detective Stories*. "Too Many Clues,"
from April 1937, is narrated by witty
young hotel manager Pete Truett. When
his house detective is arrested for
murder, Truett smells fish and does
something about it. This is the last
of the Hunters in my pulp collection,
and one of the all-around best. I
would be very surprised if there were
not more, some perhaps even better.

†

The Tod Hunter photo on the first
page of this article ran with a short
biographical note in the August 22,
1930, *Detective Fiction Weekly*. Hunter, it says, was born in Topeka, Kan-
sas, on the first day of 1897, a direct descendant of a petty officer on
the Mayflower. Before turning to
writing he was an actor, a bellhop,
a bank teller, a cook, and a football
coach. He is said to be the author
of several books outside the mystery
field, including a history of cart-
ography and a psychiatric jokebook
called *Mind Chasms*.

All of this seems to have very
little to do with W.T. Ballard. He
was born six years later in Ohio,
claiming noble descent. If he ever
held any of the jobs above, he apparently never told anyone, and he is
not credited with having published a
really oddball book until 1967.

And that was where I stood a
couple of years ago. I had plenty of
crazy clues, but nothing to rea-ly tie
them all together.

And I was still standing one-
legged in that same spot three weeks
ago when *it* arrived.

†

My parents departed January 19 on

TOO MANY CLUES

By Tod Hunter

a do-it-yourself tour of Australia and New Zealand. "Anything we can bring you?" they asked.

So. I ran off seventeen copies of my want list and asked them to drop it off at used book shops along the way.

And that they did.

Of the fifty or sixty titles on the list, only one turned up immediately: a 1st U.K. in dust wrapper of *Sinners and Shrouds* by Jonathan Latimer. This they purchased for $8 Australian, a decent price. But the real find of the trip was not on the list at all.

At the bottom I had added a note about the rumored Nero Wolfe comic book. No one knew anything about the comic, but a lady in Melbourne remembered an old paperback she thought was interesting because it was *like* Nero Wolfe. Well, since she only wanted a dollar for it, and they weren't having much luck with the list, they picked it up and mailed it back with the Latimer book.

I do not flabbergast easily, but I did it in spades when I opened that package and found *An Orchid for a Killer*. The cover you can see for yourself. It's an odd-sized paperback, wider and shorter than modern American books. There are 156 pages. On the copyright page it says simply "Copyright 1948 by Kookaburra Books, Ltd., Melbourne, Australia."

There was only one thing to do. I read it. First off, I can tell you this book was not written by W.T. Ballard. I'm no Stout expert, but I've read enough of the Wolfe series to know Archie Goodwin pretty well. And this is him. Only in this book his name is Archie Goodman, and some of the people in his life are Inspector Crater, Perly Snubbins, Paul Panzer, Franklin Horstman, and Hans the cook. His boss is a fat guy named Titus Lyon.

†

Internal evidence suggests the story was written in the very late thirties or very early forties. This may explain why it never saw print in the U.S.

Titus Lyon's client in this one, for the first time in his (or Wolfe's) career, is Japanese. Lyon at first refuses to see him and lectures Archie on the evils of the Sino-Japanese War. But next morning at 9:30 a messenger delivers a rare Japanese orchid, and Lyon comes all the way down from his plant rooms to see it. Archie knows he's hooked.

Lyon agrees to see the man, Hiroshi Toda, that evening. Initially Lyon is quite cool, but he is eventually won over by Toda's knowledge and appreciation of food and orchids..

Toda, it develops, is the owner of the finest Japanese restaurant in New

York. Chinese restaurant owners, he says, have rallied the tongs against him and he has been subjected to every sort of harassment. The police have shown neither sympathy nor results. Now the tongs are threatening his life.

Lyon would turn him down flat, of course, if not for the orchid. But as it is, he agrees to consider the matter overnight.

Next morning they learn that Ling Pao, the man Toda believed to be the leader of the tong, was dismembered during the night with a Japanese sword.

Lyon sits at his desk all through his plant time, staring with nearly closed eyes at the orchid. Archie enjoys his struggle, knowing Lyon would like to return the flower and disclaim all responsibility to Toda. But Archie knows he won't, because he wants the orchid too much.

I have checked the oepning lines of *An Orchid for a Killer* with the opening of every story in the Wolfe series, including "Bitter End." None matches up, so it looks like *An Orchid for a Killer* is an original work.

The book begins:

> What Titus Lyon tells me, and what he doesn't tell me, never depends, as far as I can make out, on the relevant circumstances. It depends on what he had to eat at the last meal, the kind of

shirt and tie I am wearing, how well my shoes are shined, and so forth.

†

But for the names, *An Orchid for a Killer* is true to the Wolfe canon in every detail. Archie rounds up visitors, Panzer works behind Archie's back, Inspector Crater interrupts dinner and Lt. Rowclift stutters. The story has some nice moments. Lyon tangles with the FBI when they try to force him off the case. Archie has a hot time persuading the tong to visit Lyon's office. Hans has a fit when Toda takes over his kitchen. Archie decides to marry Toda's niece and open a tea house.

I can think of nothing short of WWII that could have prevented the publication of *An Orchid for a Killer*. My only guess is that the book was slated to appear some time in 1942 but was shelved after Pearl Harbor.

How and why the book surfaced in Australia I can't even guess. There's always the chance it was published without Stout's knowledge or consent, but that would not explain the use of the name Tod Hunter.

And that's the problem. I don't know if I have solved the mystery or deepened it.

One thing for sure. That Tod Hunter photo looks different to me now.

?

[This article originally appeared in the fanzine *Fast One* in March 1982, in the 45th mailing of DAPA-EM.]

Case in Point: Gorky Park
By George N. Dove

Many readers of Martin Cruz Smith's *Gorky Park* undoubtedly approached the novel with a sense of curiosity motivated by the opportunity for a rare view of policemen as they live and work behind the Iron Curtain. Such interest could be especially strong with a reader of the police procedural stories of Ed McBain, James McClure, and Maj Sjöwall and Per Wahlöö, who might long ago have concluded that policemen are much the same throughout the western world and who would now jump at the chance for an authentic picture of the communist cop at the very center of things in Moscow itself. After all, we have never bet a Russian policeman close up in the police procedural and may thus feel ourselves deprived in comparison with the readers of tales of espionage, who runs into Russian agents on almost every page.

One thing is certain: anybody looking into *Gorky Park* for a first intimate view of the hitherto hidden world of totalitarian menace is sure to be surprised, because what he will find is a familiar atmosphere in terms of police attitudes, politics, enforcement methods, and even the character of the policeman-hero and his problems. As long as the scene of *Gorky Park* is with the police in Moscow, the habitual reader of procedural stories should feel quite at home. The basic change in the direction of this story comes about after the arrest of the policeman-protagonist, Arkady Renko, resulting in his imprisonment in the country safe house and the extended contest of wills between him and Major Pribluda of the KGB. When the account moves to New York, the familiar world of the police environment is left behind, replaced by the totally different ambiance of the story of international intrigue.

The first three quarters of the book, though (the section entitled "Moscow"), is essentially standard police procedural formula. The author gives us an early signal of his intentions when he tells us that Chief Investigator Renko usually deals with unimaginative murders devoid of finesse and disassociated from criminal organization, the kind of crime committed by the lone drunk who hits his beloved over the head with an ax (p. 10 [all page numbers refer to the paperback reprint, Ballantine, 1982]). Here at the beginning of the story, however, is something dramatically different: three mutilated corpses under the frozen snow in a busy public park, a totally exceptional kind of murder. We can regard this as a suggestion of intent because it represents the situational

formula of the procedural story, the one exciting exception in
an otherwise humdrum existence. Fictional policemen in America
and Europe have always complained about the dreariness and
boredom of their professional lives, even while engaged in the
big exceptional case that is the subject of the current story.
   The antagonism between the Moscow police and the KGB,
which develops early in the story and constitutes a major plot
element, also follows a familiar pattern. Local police forces
customarily resent national secret or semi-secret agencies,
like the FBI in America, "Sepo" in the Swedish stories of
Sjöwall and Wahlöö, and BOSS, the Bureau of State Security in
the South African stories of James McClure. The reader already
familiar with these rivalries will not be surprised when the
appearance of police Chief Investigator Renko and Major Pribluda of the KGB at the murder scene is accompanied by a sharp
exchange over the question of jurisdiction, or that the·KGB
man takes over the investigation with much the same kind of
arrogance as FBI agents use in American stories. A few pages
later, when the KGB men have done a good job of spoiling the
evidence and have left the scene to the Moscow cops, Renko·en-
joys at least partial retaliation when he orders his team
photographer to take some new, pictures of the corpses; the
ones done by the KGB are good for souvenirs, says the Chief
Inspector, "but not for police work" (p. 8), a slur on their
lack of professionalism that is reminiscent of the contempt
of the Swedish police for the bungling "Sepo." Finally, there
is the KGB spy planted on Renko's team in the person of a new
detective assigned to him; Renko identifies him as a plant,
gladly feeds him enough mis-information to confuse the KGB,
and finally gives him a time-consuming assignment that is cal-
culated to keep him out of the way for a considerable period.
This KGB plant, who is not very bright, recalls Detective
Catalano in Dorothy Uhnak's *The Investigation*, another obtuse
spy placed on a squad for political purposes, and Joe Peters'
method of dealing with him in that novel is very much like
Renko's handling of the KGB plant.
   Police attitudes in *Gorky Park* are not drastically different from those in the western procedurals. The contempt
of the plainclothes men for the uniformed branch is even
stronger in this story, because ordinary patrol activities in
Moscow are carried on by the militia, whom Muscovites regard
as an ·army of occupation, who are farm boys enlisted out of
the Army, and who are generally classed in the public mind as
unclutured ýokels and brutes. They remind us of the beat-
pounders west of·the Iron Curtain in the care they exercise
to avoid making each other look bad, by the simple expedient
of not reporting any more crime than is absolutely necessary.
The attitude of the Moscow police toward the reliability of
witnesses is also strongly reminiscent of the general distrust
of witnesses expressed by policemen in fiction: their memories
fade after one day, Renko tells another character, and after
three months they can be.persuaded that they have seen whatever the investigator wants them to see.
   The Moscow police are not handicapped by the necessity
for respecting the rights of civilians to the extent that the
western police are, but their methods of investigation seem
otherwise consistent with those practiced by fictional police
detectives everywhere. Their laboratory work is apparently
competent, especially as it is applied to identification by

means of protein analysis of human hairs, and by microscopic
examination and analysis (pp. 80, 112). When he needs special
expertise, however, Arkady Renko follows the same policy as do
most other European detectives in procedural stories, turning
for help to an outside agency, in this case the Soviet Academy's
Institute of Ethnology, which has perfected the technique of
rebuilding human heads from skulls. European detectives seem
willing to depend on civilian expertise as Renko does here;
Americans tend to rely exclusively upon police laboratory work.
    Besides these parallels in the workings of the police mind
and the methodology of law enforcement, *Gorky Park* has a familiar ring in the person of its protagonist. Arkady Renko is
a capable policeman who tends to be modest about his achieve-
ments, but he is also a human being with a highly developed
sense of justice who once persuaded the city prosecutor to re-
open a case because he was not satisfied with the original
verdict. He reminds us more than a little of Nicolas Free-
ling's Inspector Van der Valk, especially in his cultural level;
Van der Valk could quote Baudelaire, but Renko can quote an
obscure Russian poet who is now out of favor with the communist
party (p. 174). Like several other police detectives, he has
marital problems: his marriage is in severe trouble as the
novel opens and breaks down as the story progresses. One interesting difference in this case lies in the fact that in so
many accounts police marriages are ruined by a wife's insis-
tence that her husband get out of police work, but Zoya Renko
wants Arkady to advance politically by becoming an active
Party member and getting himself assigned as investigator for
the Central Committee. Partly because of his unsatisfying
marriage, Arkady Renko falls in love with the suspect Irina
Asanova, and in so doing he joins the considerable number of
his western colleagues who carry on love affairs with suspects, witnesses, and victims.
    In his approach to the business of detection, Arkady Renko
is considerably more discerning and perceptive than most.
After he and Detective Pavlovich have badgered a stubborn wit-
ness without success, the two policemen go out to lunch, but
not until Renko has placed a bottle of vodka in the suspect's
hands, tacitly daring him to have the few drinks that will
lower his defenses. "You're a subtle bastard," says Pavlovich
(p. 127).
    The atmosphere of the police procedural disappears in the
section of the story called "Chatura," in which Renko, now
under arrest, is held in isolation while the agents of the KGB
try to coax and bully a confession out of him. Arkady sur-
vives this ordeal partly because of his own personal integrity
and partly because of his ingrained police orientation. To
the threats of his tormentors who try to force him into confession regarding the facts of the case, his response is the
standard trustworthy cop reply: "You have my report" (p. 316).
The third and last section, entitled "New York," is far removed from the element of normal police work and raises the
tempo of the action into a bloody holocaust typical of the
hazardous world of Robert Ludlum, Ken Follett, and Frederick
Forsyth.
    The first part of the novel, however, in which the Moscow
police are at work in the normal environment, follows the
police procedural pattern as it has been standardized by
stories about cops in London, Stockholm, America, and else-
(Continued on page ...)

Black and White and Dead
James McClure's South Africa
By Fred Isaac

Traditionally, the mystery has held itself apart from most of the concerns of our everyday lives. The suspense and spy forms are exempted from this to the extent that they have sometimes used "ordinary" people thrust into dangerous circumstances. In Britain there is also the legacy of the hero turned super-hero, a line that goes back at least to Bulldog Drummond and led logically to appearances by many of the great detectives as spies, counter-spies, and war workers from 1938 to 1945. Since then, with increasing but generally unremarkable frequency, our genre has usually eschewed real-life situations. The political leader at a party is far more likely to become victim than killer, and, in the case of his actually being the culprit, the explanation is personal rather than public.

In much the same way, social problems have been avoided for the most part; when treated at all, the handling has been delicate. Race, one of the most problematic of them, has been avoided throughout the century. Prior to 1950 there were only three major non-white detectives: Charlie Chan, Napoleon Bonaparte, and, stretching a point, Mr. Moto. It is notable that all of them worked essentially alone and that their activities were usually confined to geographical areas in which they were inconspicuous--Hawaii, Australia's Outback, and pre-war China. While all of them were granted status and were successful as characters, the impression lingers that race was in some measure a handicap. Bony, for instance, relied on his absolute success for his eminence on the force, and we are reminded of this fact in all of the novels.

Since 1950 the two subjects of race and politics have increasingly become part of our genre. In the mid-1960's and after, Per Wahlöö and Maj Sjöwall levelled direct criticism at the socialist government of their native Sweden. The lenient judges and deteriorating life styles of American cities have received criticism from various sides, but seldom as bitter or as constant as from Elizabeth Linington, whose Lieutenant Luis Mendoza is constantly frustrated. Mendoza also reflects a slight broadening of the spectrum of heroes, being a third-generation American hispanic. His view of the downtown areas of Los Angeles shows a deteriorating city, but this is pleasant fare compared with the Harlem of Chester Himes. Himes's team of Jones and Johnson, big, black, and mean, gave readers a taste of real Ghetto life, where death and depravity are all around and ordinary folks live on the very edge of violence. In his later Gideon books, John Creasey includes short views of London's race problems, visible signs of the need for change. Before the saddened but helpless eyes of Gideon, the Africans, West Indians, Indians, and Pakistanis became the majority inhabitants of some areas of London, while the business and political leaders turned their backs.

The most auspicious book in the entire mystery form prior to James McClure's arrival was John Ball's *In the Heat of the Night*. That book, and the movie made from it (which kept remarkably close to the original), introduced black detective Virgil Tibbs. While in his later appearances Tibbs has not made an issue of his race, this book approached prejudice through detection more closely than any previous novel. The relation between Tibbs and Chief Gillespie, as it changes from hatred and wariness to a mutual respect, makes this one of the few truly social novels of detection yet written.

Even so, it is hard to imagine early readers of James McClure's *Steam Pig* not being surprised and even shocked at its contents. The *Steam Pig* and all of the books that have succeeded it are set in South Africa, the unhappy land of Apartheid, and McClure has used them as a soapbox on which to become an outspoken critic of the people and the government. Since 1967, McClure has blended police procedural mysteries with a unique fury extending past the official policy to a deep anger at the people who tolerate the situation.

Many of us tend to skip the background commentary in many of the books we read; with McClure, this is indeed a mistake. His first view of Lieutenant Tromp Kramer finds the hero writing up a report on a murder in Peacevale, the black township outside the city. As he writes, a prisoner--we never learn who--is being tortured in the next room. We never know why; it is just a part of life. The report itself is of little interest, but Kramer's thoughts give an early indication of his attitudes and those of his superior:

> An inquest was nothing compared to a court case.

> Shantytown folk always relished a bit of rough justice.

> The Colonel would not bother to glance through the report when he got it; if you've read one Bantu murder you've read the lot, he invariably observed. [*The Steam Pig*, chapter 2]

There are, of course, several responses to this horror. Kramer could object to the treatment of the prisoner--but he does not. He could agree with it as he seems to pass off the "rough justice" of the poor blacks--but he does not do that either, at least not for us readers to see. Instead, his reaction is a bland acquiescence, a benign awareness. He implies, here and elsewhere, that while he is not completely at ease with things as they are, his security and his position in society are at stake and a low profile is the best policy.

There is a unique logic at work in this position. It is made explicit--or as much so as possible--by Kramer's relations with his partner-assistant, Bantu Sergeant Mickey Zondi. Zondi arrives at the apartment of the dead woman after Kramer, and he awakens the lieutenant from a nap. In this scene the depth and contradiction of the two men's relationship is established. Kramer first notices the small attributes that fascinate him about Zondi.

> The laugh never seemed to come from him, it was too big a sound.
> ... The clothes ... all were second hand ideas from a second
> hand shop. The walk was pure Chicago, yet no black was per-
> mitted to see a gangster film. No, here was an original....
> Zondi walked that way because he thought that way. [*The Steam
> Pig*]

Having gotten Kramer's attention, Zondi sits at the victim's desk, opens the envelope he has brought with him from the laboratory, and studies the pictures. Against all regulations, he asks nothing of Kramer.

> Even a dead white woman had laws to protect her from primitive
> lust....
> "You want to get me into trouble, hey."
> Zondi ignored him.... "A good woman," he said. "She could
> have given many sons."
> "Is that all you think about?" asked Kramer, and they both
> laughed. Zondi was an incorrigible pelvis man. [*The Steam Pig*]

It is the laugh that binds the two men and makes us care for them through their stories. It signifies the sharing of a special point of view and their bond against the world that threatens them. It is an open act of unrecognized friendship, the most lasting sign of their closeness in opposition to both law and custom.

Once identified, the attachment can be seen in a variety of ways throughout the series, even though Kramer cannot even recognize it. For instance, when the Widow Fourie, Kramer's mistress, moves into a house, Zondi helps with the transferral and is rewarded by a large load of nearly new discards, which Mickey can either use or sell. The method is unorthodox to us, but it protects both the superiority of the white donor and the pride of the black recipient. As Zondi puts it, "She knew how to give so it didn't hurt to take from her" [*Snake*].

The other side of the relationship can be seen in *The Gooseberry Fool*. Having sent Zondi into the bush in an official car to find a man, Kramer finds that Zondi is in the hospital. As Zondi knows, "being allowed the initiative was a true compliment," but the worry now is that the relationship is destroyed or, perhaps worse, uncovered. When Kramer visits Zondi's wife Miriam at their hovel in Peacevale, he asks her whether his superiors "think I'm a Kaffir-lover?" If so, then both Kramer and Zondi have lost the freedom of action which they need in order to operate effectively.

Paired with others, Kramer and Zondi protect each other and once more reinforce their togetherness. Kramer, for his part, is more high-handed and imperious with other whites beneath him, and he is insubordinate to his police superiors. There are a number of assumptions which can be drawn from his dealings with other whites. Young white officers who want to rise in the force must first of all be told what to do, in the same way most blacks are. In addition, they should be scared off of Kramer's turf, either by the gruesomeness of the business or by Kramer's manner. If they disregard the lieutenant's orders, they are subject to discipline, which will put them back. Kramer's superiors, who consider him overly independent, pass him off as questionable, which gives him--and, by extension, Zondi--the opportunity to work as he sees fit. Zondi takes pride is his own status as a policeman--and also in Kramer's trust in him, as we have already seen. He, too, is mindful of their mutual dependence, and his actions with others demonstrate this. When, for instance, Nxumalo, the black aide to the coroner's office, makes disparaging remarks about his superiors, Zondi chuckles but does not respond in kind. On the occasions when he questions servants, he slips easily into general comments on the strange ways of the "Bosses," but he seldom directly speaks of Kramer and his mannerisms. The thoughtfulness which this suggests is a basic part of Zondi's personality. With whites the problem of distance is, of course, far greater. While "even" the dead Theresa LeRoux of *The Steam Pig* was protected by her whiteness (although, as we shall see, this is subject to change), the real reason for the laws is the separation of the living whites from black intrusion. Driving around Trekkersburg in *Blood of an Englishman*, Zondi obtains two rare opportunities to break through the barriers. When he and Kramer visit Mrs. Westford, Zondi mistakes her retarded son for the gardener. Timmy, who has been protected, greets him as "Mr. African," and the pair then talk almost as equals. Later, when he and Tish, the hairdresser's assistant, are waiting for Kramer outside the Bradshaw house, he calls her "madam" and she tells him she is uncomfortable with the title. His one-word comment is "Impossible." Significantly, though, he does not remonstrate with her, and the reaction is a thought and not verbalized aloud. Thus he protects himself and does not hurt her feelings.

In their professional relations with other police, Kramer and Zondi are both circumspect and devious. All of the books include examples of the mixture of their obedience to the letter of the rules and their personal evasion of their spirit. Perhaps the best of all is in *The Gooseberry Fool*. On their way to investigate Hugo Swart's death, the lieutenant gives Zondi the car keys. "Zondi would have thanked him but at that moment Constable van der Poel had come up to them, so instead he gave a sulky shrug and shuffled off...." Here is the essence of the conflict between the professional and personal sides of their camaraderie. Without the intrusion of the young white officer, Zondi may have thanked Kramer quietly. Or, as happens between them, Kramer might have made a crack about Zondi's reckless driving. Or any of a number of sly bits of conversation could have taken place. The effect of an outsider is to seal the two parts of the men off. From then on, care must be taken to conceal the private world from view. This is usually easier to do. When the pair is found disobeying orders, or when Zondi is caught where he should not be, Kramer refuses the blame. In *Blood of an Englishman*, Colonel Muller excuses Kramer on the basis of stress and overwork for allowing Zondi to go into a white holding. Kramer, in turn, says he was unaware of the problem. "Hell, Colonel, he's only a Kaffir, isn't he? What do you think?" The persistence of this situation suggests that Kramer can only protect himself by giving Zondi the blame, while Zondi's race is reason enough to exempt him, if not exonerate him from responsibility.

One final point should be made in regard to their behavior

on the job. Kramer's solicitude for Zondi only goes so far,
as we know. But he has other uses for his concern. In *The
Sunday Hangman* Zondi is suffering from an untreated problem
resulting from his being shot in the leg. Out in the bush,
the wound is painful, but Kramer sends him to a village to ask
about the latest hanging. When Dr. Strydom, the pathologist,
asks about the need, Kramer interrupts, saying "The lazy bug-
ger needs a walk." In fact, Zondi's pain is great, and he
needs time to get over it. Secondly, his knowledge of the
bush and its people allows him to gather the village children,
who have hidden to watch the police, much more quickly than a
white constable could have. Finally, as a black, he can talk
to the people without unduly frightening them. Later, as the
case continues, Kramer realizes the severity of Zondi's problem and effectively removes him from the case to recover and
be treated. To assume Kramer's callousness and lack of feel-
ing is, therefore, to misread entirely the conflicting feelings and the deceptive nature of his comments.
    There is a certain irony about the plots of the half-
dozen Kramer-and-Zondi novels. While the racial aspect exists
throughout the series in the personal and inter-personal relations and thoughts, the murders are usually without racial
overtones. In only one book does the separation of races become a major plot element. In *The Steam Pig* Theresa LeRoux is
a "coloured" woman who has passed--entered the white world although her parents are not white. The fact of this unauthorized
situation might have gone unnoticed but for her mother, who
comes to Kramer to claim the body. Kramer himself does not
realize that the older woman is not white until, searching for
her at the bus station, he sees her leaving the non-white rest
room. Though the fact is not crucial in one sense, it changes
the direction of Kramer's comprehension of the dead woman's
character, and this leads to the ultimate uncovering of her
manipulation and to Kramer's solution of her murder.
    In the other books in the series, there are several run-
ning investigations, some involving white deaths, others non-
white, either coloured or black murders. As in the rest of
the social order of South Africa, these are kept apart, almost
hermetically separated from each other. This suggests two
things to the attentive reader. First, that the author has
attempted to write procedural stories to the greatest extent
possible, rather than tying a number of disparate plot devices
together in a traditional manner. At the same time, the great
distance between the various segments of the nation's people
is emphasized by the force of Apartheid. Kramer and Zondi
work together, but also separately on a number of occasions,
as if to once more remind the reader of the high priority the
government places on the regulation of inter-racial mixing,
even on the professional level. There is, in fact, something
subversive in the Widow Fourie's offer that Zondi and his family can move into her house in her absence--even if only to
protect it from intruders. The additional irony is that most
of those who would burglarize it are black.
    Moving from the solely racial aspects of the books to
their larger political context, there is a strong measure of
fear and resultant caution, as well as hate, in McClure's
books. This can also, and perhaps better, be seen in *Rogue
Eagle*, the only novel thus far without Kramer and Zondi. This
novel recounts one mission by Finbar Buchanan, a British agent

living in Lesotho. Hearing of a gathering of members of the
banned Broederband (Afrikaner Brotherhood), he investigates
and finds them plotting to overthrow the prime minister of
South Africa for his lenient (!) policies on race. His unlikely ally in foiling the plot is Wolraad Steyn, son of one
of the plotters and the rogue of the title. The point here is
that the need for security from the majority is being fought
from the Right by those who fear the collapse of the nation if
present laws are loosened. (On the other side is the black
position, most notably espoused by the African National Con-
gress, which has for several years been at war with the author-
ities.) Finbar is ultimately successful, but casualties include a white doctor, all of his patients, and his hospital in
the bush, as a result of an attack by the white group including Wolraad Steyn's father.

Kramer and Zondi have not yet been involved in a conflict
with the law to this extent. In a few cases, though, the
security laws have been in evidence. *The Gooseberry Fool*,
with all of its nearly open hostility to societal race policies, is also the most directly political in a non-racial way.
At first, Hugo Swart's murder seems straightforward enough.
On the basis of his first investigation, Kramer sends Zondi to
bring back Thomas Shabalala, Swart's servant, for questioning.
But after Zondi leaves (the "true compliment" mentioned earlier), Kramer is unaccountably removed and reassigned to a
traffic death. Unhappy and troubled, Kramer privately follows
some leads and concludes by tying Swart to the car crash. In
the meantime, Zondi retrieves Thomas and, on the way back to
the city, is run off the road. The crash kills Shabalala and
lands Zondi in the hospital, comatose from head wounds. Kramer
is both stunned and angered by the non-random nature of the
events. His efforts show that the Bureau of State Security
(the very real and infamous BOSS) had planted Swart to do
undercover work. When he overstepped his authority, he was
killed by one of the people he was blackmailing. To cover the
BOSS connection, the agency has Kramer removed and Zondi run
down to keep the problem quiet. That Kramer's accident victim
is also Swart's killer is an unlucky coincidence (and literary
license). But the graver crime, to Zondi, is never questioned;
after all, next time it could be the "right" thing for Boss to
do.

Following in the footsteps of Alan Paton, James McClure
has continued the tradition of serious criticism of South
Africa through its racial and political systems. Happily, he
is no longer alone. In two novels since 1979, Wessel Ebersohn,
who still lives in South Africa, has given us a second figure
in the fight against crime and other ills. Yudel Gordon, a
professional psychologist who also works with the police, began his career in *A Lonely Place to Die*. In that book he went
to a small bush town to clear a retarded black man of the
death of his lifetime employer, the "Old Boss" of the area.
While not as direct as McClure, the book has several vignettes
which examine closely the social interaction of the races in
small towns. The second book, *Divide the Night*, confronts the
ethics of murder and race in a unique and powerful way. In
part, the novel examines the mind of shopkeeper Johnny Weizman,
whose defense is that he has a right (absolute in South Africa)
to kill intruders into his store and home. It also ranges into

the underground, where guerillas hide from the government, and
into the torture cells of the police to watch suspected terror-
ists undergo "questioning." Yudel's horror is increased by
the stoicism of his friend Freek, a policeman who sees his
role much as Tromp Kramer does--to capture the guilty and to
protect the society from depradation. While Freek does not
take active part in the work seen by Yudel, it is clear that
his unconcern is conditioned by many hours as an active parti-
cipant.

And, just as McClure has written *Rogue Eagle*, Ebersohn's
other book to date (published between the Gordon investigations) puts a spotlight on the guresome nature of the society.
Look Back in Anger tells of a young black leader, a fugitive
from the police, who has been captured and is now enduring his
last days in a room. Surrounded by his captors, Sam Bhengu is
naked, refused food, clothing, sleep, and even the right to
urinate. During the days of his slow death he relives his
life, the people he has known and loved, and the growth of his
passion for freedom. Finally, when the police realize that he
will trouble them no longer, they put him in a van and begin
to take him--we are not told where. Seen entirely through the
eyes and memories of Sam Bhengu (a fictionalized Steven Biko),
the book is riveting, haunting, and pathetic.

Thus today there are really two writers using police and
crime as the vehicle for deep and touching criticism of the
people and social structure of South Africa today. To quote a
line from Alan Paton's *Ah, but Your Land Is Beautiful*, the
hearts of the inhabitants "are growing too hard." Yet amid
the brutality the human qualities persist, and writers acute
enough have brought them to our attention.

(Continued from page 11) *(Continued from page 11)* where. Of course, *Gorky Park* is a
story about Russian policemen written by an American, but it
is another reminder that the procedural formula is universal
in its application and influence.

(Continued from page 44) *Grow the Dollars* is the pick of the
crop. You don't have to be green-thumbed to like it. (Jane
S. Bakerman)

Barbara D'Amato. *The Hands of Healing Murder*. Charter, 1980.

A book I'd been looking forward to reading for some time
and, frankly, something of a disappointment. I guessed the
murderer (well, who else could it have been, for goodness
sake!) and found the whole thing rather slow and mechanical.
The first quarter of the book showed much promise, but it
rather fell away, and the impossible crime really wasn't all
that impossible. (Bob Adey)

Stuart Kaminsky. *Never Cross a Vampire*. St. Martin's, 1980.

P.I. Toby Peters, as many of you will know, carries out
his investigations among the real-life celebrities of the Los
Angeles of forty years ago. All this had led me to expect a
rather gimicky, name-dropping sort of book and little else.
But not so. Certainly Peters' clients are Bela Lugosi (who's
being threatened) and William Faulkner (who's being wrongfully
(Continued on page 22)

British Murder and British Detective Fiction
By Earl F. Bargainnier

One of the major criticisms directed at traditional or
"classical" British detective fiction is its unreality. It
has been described as too cosy, too much concerned with gather-
ings at country houses, too conservatively middle class, avoid-
ing the mean streets and violence inherent in actual crime.
From Raymond Chandler's "The Simple Art of Murder" to Colin
Watson's *Snobbery with Violence*, the attacks have been so consistent that they have practically developed into an accepted
truism: classical British detective fiction is an artificial,
mechanical form of escapist fiction with no relation to reality.
        For those who unquestioningly accept the truism, I suggest
an examination of J.H.H. Gaute and Robin Odell's *Murderers'
Who's Who* (Montreal: Optimum Publishing Company, Ltd., 1979),
an encyclopedia of famous true murderers and unexplained
deaths. Although it is international in scope, the emphasis
is upon British and American cases. Reading it casually, I
was struck by the number of real British murders which sounded
like so much of the British detective fiction I have read.
Eliminating the few works that are or seem to be directly
founded upon real crimes--for example, Nicholas Blake's *A
Tangled Web* (1956), admittedly based upon the 1912 John Williams case, and H.R.F. Keating's "Gup" (1978), which must owe
something to the 1928 Benjamin Knowles case, the change of
setting from the Gold Coast to India and other incidentals
aside--the fact remains that much British detective fiction is
paralleled by similar crimes in British life.
        Intrigued by the similarities and parallels, I have
categorized all of the murders included by Gaute and Odell
from Great Britain, Canada, South Africa, Australia, New Zealand, and India, as well as those involving British subjects
in other parts of Africa, Japan, and the Caribbean. The total
is 240, and they fall into three definable groups, plus a
fourth miscellaneous group:

Family Murders	72
Murders for Gain	67
Sexual Murders	53
Others	48
TOTAL	240

Of course, many of the family murders--as in fiction--are the
result of greed or sex, but the limitation used here is that

the murder is of a family member by another member (Sidney
Fox, 1929) or of one of the members of an adulterous triangle
by one or both of the other two (Dr. H.H. Crippen, 1910).
Murder for gain may result during a robbery (Jack Goldenberg,
1924) or from some more complicated plan to obtain money
through insurance, illegal business transactions, fraud, or
confidence scheme (Nurse Waddingham, 1935)--but not through
inheritance, which is considered a form of family murder.
Likewise, sexual murder is varied, but for this grouping
does not include members of the same family; it ranges from
psychopathic rape-murder (The Moors Murders, 1963-65) to one
lover killing another (John Thorne, 1924). The miscellaneous
group of murders--surprisingly the smallest--results from in-
sanity, kidnapping, revenge, feuds, fights, gangsterism, and
sheer anger, as well as those which are seemingly without
motive (Alfred Rouse, 1930) and those which are unsolved. The
most famous of the last are, without question, the five murders of Jack the Ripper (1888) which have provided the basis
for so many fictional works, most notably Marie Belloc
Loundes's *The Lodger* (1913) and Thomas Burke's "The Hands of
Mr. Ottermole" (1931).

Though gain and sex are often motives in family murders,
when they are removed from the family environment they seem
better suited to the thriller than to the detective story, and
the same is true, excepting revenge, for the miscellaneous
group of murders. (This is a broad generalization, and I myself can think of dozens of exceptions in classical British
detective fiction, but most of those exceptions replace the
family with some group which serves in the identical function
of providing a closed circle of suspects; the cast of a play,
the passengers on a ship, the masters at a school, the employees of an advertising firm, etc.) There is less doubt as
to the identity of the perpetrator of a murder resulting from
robbery or a confidence scheme than there is for a family murder where the relationships and motives are so much more complex than simple greed; this holds true both in real cases and
in fiction, and the "action" is the pursuit and capture of the
identifiable suspect. The situation is reversed with sexual
murder. Since it nearly always results from some psychological
imbalance, solving such a case requires identifying a person
who may present a "normal" facade. The difference between
non-family sexual murder and one within a family is that in
the first the murderer may be any one of thousands of people,
whereas in the second the suspects are limited to a very few.
The Peter Griffiths case (1948) required the fingerprinting of
the entire adult male population of Blackburn, England, to
discover the sex-murderer of a little girl; Griffiths' prints
were number 46,253. Such effort is unnecessary when one
family member kills another, but one would have difficulty
creating a classical detective novel from the Griffiths case--
though it might make an interesting police procedural.

That British detective fiction is most often centered on
family relationships is indisputable. It is so to a much
greater degree than the thirty percent such real murders account for in Gaute and Odell. The problem for the detective
is to find the person who has disrupted the family "community"
by disposing of one or more members. Whatever the motive,'
since a family murder involves the most closely knot of social
groups, the detective writer is provided with all sorts of

misdirection in the various relationships among the family members. The principal difference between real family murders and those of fiction is that rarely in actuality do four or five members of a family have a reason for killing one member, whereas authors can arrange their plots with that many or more. In classical British detective fiction the victim is often a patriarchal figure, who is controlling the lives of the other family members: withholding money, preventing marriages, demanding surservience in any number of ways. But in the vast majority of real family murders the victim is an unwanted spouse removed by his or her marriage-partner (of course, such murders also appear frequently in fiction). What is most significant is, to repeat, the number of family murders in British detective fiction, as in real life. The obvious technical reason for their popularity is the closed circle of suspects they provide the author, but they also indicate that British writers are aware, consciously or unconsciously, of what type of murder is most prevalent in their country.

It should also be noted that some of the devices so often criticized as artificial in classical detective fiction have parallels in actual cases. One is the murderer's making a slip of the tongue and thus convicting himself. Consider the case of John Thomas Straffen, accused of strangling a child in 1951. "Interviewed at Broadmoor, Straffen completely gave himself away, saying, 'I did not kill the little girl on the bicycle', even before he was asked." Or Ethel Lillie Major, who, when questioned by the police about her husband's death in 1934, said, "I did not know that my husband died of strychnine poisoning," and, on the police replying that strychnine had not been mentioned, added, "Oh, I'm sorry. I must have made a mistake." Indeed; she was hanged! The fictional murderer who deliberately intrudes himself into the investigation of his murder has become a cliché, perhaps because Agatha Christie used it so often (*The ABC Murders, The Pale Horse, Death in the Clouds, Three Act Tragedy,* and others). However, she used it no more often than it has actually happened (Jack Goldenberg, 1924; Frederick Field, 1931; Reginald Buckfield, 1943; Neville George Heath, 1946; John George Haigh, 1949; Herbert Mills, 1951; Peter Manuel, 1958; Graham Young, 1971). Young, in fact, used the same poison as the murderer in Christie's *The Pale Horse*--thallium--and the novel predated the real case.

It sometimes may seem that detective writers set out to think up the most bizarre murders possible. Ngaio Marsh, Georgette Heyer, Edmund Crispin, and John Dickson Carr come immediately to mind. But they have their equals among actual murderers. For example, in 1943 Eric Brown attached a land mine to his invalid father's wheelchair--with predictably spectacular results. More "cosy" was Major H.R. Armstrong's serving arsenical tea scones to a business rival in 1921, an attempt at murder which would fit into any number of novels. Equally bizarre are the ways murders have attempted to dispose of their victim's corpses: bodies hacked into pieces, mailed in trunks, dipped in acid, cemented under hearthstones, burned, buried (the body of Mamie Stuart, killed in 1920, was not found until 1961, three years after her murderer had died at the age of 78), and even thrown into the sea from an airplane (Brian Hume, 1949). Certainly bizarre was the human arm re-

gurgitated by a captive tiger shark in Australia in 1935, resulting in identification of the victim and a trial but no
conviction. Agatha Christie was surely right to prefer poison
for her murderers' weapon. Although there are quite enough
instances of shooting, stabbing, bludgeoning, and strangula-
tion--the last nearly always by sex murderers--at least in
these famous cases poisoning is the favorite method. The
poisons most often used are arsenic and strychnine, but others
include morphine, insulin, aconitine, antimony, thallium,
prussic acid, and bacterial cultures. Murderers have attempted
to explain away the effects of poison as heat-stroke, typhoid
fever, dozing off in the bath, and, repeatedly, gastro-enteritis.
Except in the case of psychopaths who kill repeatedly, there
are few examples of the later murder so prevalent in detective
fiction, generally committed from fear of detection. Nevertheless, there is one notable instance: Richard Brinkley (1907)
realized that there were witnesses to the fake will of his
first victim and systematically set out to eliminate them, but
failed.

Parallels and similarities could be multiplied, but this
brief survey of Gauté and Odell's volume is not meant to prove
that classical British detective fiction is "realistic"; no
detective fiction--indeed, no fiction--is ultimately realistic.
Rather, it attempts to make those who so quickly dismiss "cosy"
detective fiction aware that, as far as the British are concerned, murder is frequently confined to the family--and if
the family should not be cosy, what should? Also, it shows
that some of the very elements most often attacked for arti-
ficiality are not so improbable after all. When someone says
that Dashiell Hammett is more realistic than Nicholas Blake,
that person should remember that he or she is basing that
judgment on his or her experience. There are as many country
houses in British detective fiction as mean streets in American, but each is simply a convention. The relation of con-
ventions to national differences is frequently ignored, and a
consideration of the varying forms of real murder in relation
to the detective fiction of a nation may help to prevent state-
ments which are supposed to be literary criticism from being,
as they too often are, simplistic or snide.

(Continued from page 18) arrested for murder) and there are
allusions to the Americana of the period, but for the rest
it's a perfectly good P.I. novel, well written and well plotted.
Even the use of the celebrities is quite logical and necessary
to the plot. I'll now have to go back and read its predeces-
sor, *The Howard Hughes Affair*, which I have, and locate his
first three books, which I don't. (Bob Adey)

John Lutz. *Bonegrinder*. Robert Hale, 1979 (first published
by Putnam in 1977).

Set in the Ozarks (a part of America I've visited), this
is a rivetting tale of a strange killer with the ability to
mutilate its victims and defy detection. Sheriff Billy Win-
tone, a conscientious law officer, finds that the investigation involves him in local bigotry, local politics, and local
prejudice. The description of the area is brilliant and ac-
curate, and the small-town atmosphere is perfectly captured.
(Continued on page 29)

Amazing Grace
By Bob Simpson

The art of marriage is complex enough already. House pay-
ments, relatives, and the urgency of matched shoes and purses
tangle the love relationship. Only a madman would hurl in
further complications by snuffling after crime and excitement.
So good sense suggests. But mystery fiction is brightly
jeweled by teams of husbands and wives whose enthusiasm for
the crime chase overrides their domestic routine.
A few teams are well known: The Norths, Nick and Nora
Charles, Tuppence and Tommy are classic figures all. But they
are not the only ones. Merely the best known. They represent
a staple, if minor, branch of mystery fiction popular for
years, their adventures brightening many a forgotten magazine,
remote in time.
The first series to feature the joint investigations of a
husband and wife seems to have appeared in 1912. That was at
the height of the initial craze for mystery fiction. Then
the living figure of Sherlock Holmes stood tall, and dime
novels, at 5¢ a copy, piled the news kiosk. And for 10¢ you
could provide yourself with a copy of *The Cavalier*, a thick
pulp magazine strongly slanted to women readers, in which appeared a serial part of "The Honeymoon Detectives."
The title suggests prose like syrup. It is not. It is
prose as bland as unsweetened farina. Honeymoon may shine in
the title, but intense love does not tumble the sentences. In
this series there is no lodging for high passion, high fear,
melodrama with flaming pistols and muscles knotted.
No, indeed. All is quiet here, like the voices of well-
bred matrons at a society funeral. Orderly discipline rules.
The scene is 1912 Paris, changing later in the series to
1915 New York City. Through a gentle, affluent glow, a young
couple moves--Richard and Grace Duvall. He is a private investigator, having offices on Union Square, New York City.
So great are his gifts that, for more than six months (as the
series opens), he has been attached to the personal staff of
Monsieur Lefever, Prefect of Paris.
And Grace, that lovely girl, also has the questing mind.
Sympathy rises quick in her. She is clever, impulsive, sensible. All things are possible, for she loves.
Together, this attractive pair moves through a series of
six simple mystery adventures. These were written by Frederic
Arnold Kummer under the pseudonym Arnold Fredericks.

Frederick Kummer (1873-1943) had a prodigious career. He married twice, had five children. Before 1900 he had been general manager of a paving-brick company and chief engineer, later general manager, of a wood-preserving company. He published extensively in these technical fields prior to taking up a literary career in 1907. Immediately he began a torrent of plays, musical comedies (one each with Sigmund Romberg and Victor Herbert), motion-picture films, and a grand opera. Between these efforts he sandwiched thirty-three books: novels, histories, mysteries. He died in Baltimore, Maryland, still working.

The six "Honeymoon Detective" adventures were published between 1912 and 1917. The stories are sequential, each referring to incidents in past cases. Grace is the heroine. By all rights, she should be half the team, collecting half the dangers, half the clues, and slightly less than half the exposure. But she manages to run away with the whole thing.

This happens in husband and wife stories. If you are Nick Charles, you can tell the story in first person and keep Nora more or less repressed. In other series where this precaution isn't taken, the wife simply seizes the lead and runs away.

It is better, for narrative unity, to have one lead character than two. The trouble with a two-part team is that, sooner or later, the wife plunges into peril and must be rescued, this being a formal convention. Since a lot of dramatic effects can be milked from her pitiful plight, the single point of view fractures here. Two action lines form. We encounter the end result often noticed in Edgar Wallace: the story has divided into such clear parts that it seems to have been written in sections and strapped together.

This structural problem occurs constantly during the Honeymoon Detective novels. There is his story and there is her story. At the end, after exhaustion has set in, it becomes Their story, a charming if inexact conclusion.

In keeping with the beliefs of 1912, Richard Duvall, the nominal lead of the series, is considered a rare genius. In the introduction to "The Mysterious Goddess," we are told:

> Duvall is unlike any other detective you have ever met in fiction; his methods are not those of *Sherlock Holmes*, or of the myriad sleuths of whom he is the prototype. They are absolutely unique.

Compared to Grace, Richard is a dullard. He spends much time being made unconscious or writhing in the hands of the fiend or muttering, "I have been uncommonly slow in this case!"

He is correct. But it is not really his fault. He is a victim of the double standard, that reverse discrimination which requires the husband to be a dullard whenever his wife gets more than 3% of the action.

Customarily, Richard goes striding off along one branch of the investigation. (Call that branch "Reason.") Grace accidentally follows a separate line. (Call this line "Intuition.") Over about three hundred pages their paths gradually close, and it turns out that each had a different end of the same rope.

Until the final pages, various improbabilities keep them from exchanging information. Finally they are united in a

moment of high peril. At this point, Richard explains all
those exceedingly strange circumstances that surround the
crime. How did the child vanish in a wide open meadow? How
do threatening letters materialize from the air? How did the
snuff-box vanish during the Ambassador's shave when no one
could possibly have approached him?

Richard tells all and is conceded to be a bright fellow
and a credit to civilization. But if it weren't for Grace ....

The series is too long to summarize all material. However,
the continuing story of the Duvalls and a few interesting adventures may be sketched out.

Matters begin in "The Honeymoon Detectives" (*The Cavalier*,
five-part serial, March 23 through April 20, 1912). Richard
Duvall, the splendid young detective, has become assistant to
the Paris Prefect of Police. While doing whatever assistants
do, he meets Grace Ellicott, victim of an elaborate conspiracy.
Her aunt has left her a fortune; her step-uncle, Count d'Este,
is determined to have it.

Things look dreary for poor Grace. Fortunately, she and
Richard have had the good sense to fall in love immediately.
And love, as it will, finds a way to foil the Count. After
which, events round off in a lovely wedding, and the blessings
of the entire Paris police are showered on "The Honeymoon Detectives."

Exactly one hour later, fictional time, "The Ivory Snuff-
Box" begins (*The Cavalier*, May 11, 1912, complete in that issue). Before Richard can kiss his bride a second time--a sud-
den crisis. With deep regrets, Monsieur Lefever must send
Richard flying to London. There, a tiny, pearl-ornamented
snuff-box has been stolen from the French Ambassador.

No one will explain to Richard why the box is so intensely
valuable. Only that its loss means that France may fall.
Maybe so. What galls Richard is not the stuffy secrecy but
that "in leaving his wife withoug even so much as a farewell
word, he had given her good reason for doubting his love for
her."

Highly annoyed, he interviews the Ambassador, traces the
snuff-box quickly through various hands and across various
corpses. By a series of deductions (just like Sherlock
Holmes, that individual he does not resemble), he determines
that the box is being smuggled back to France.

All through these adventures, he is in a fearful sweat
that Grace will never speak to him again, that she is weeping,
etc. etc.

Grace has no time to weep. She is back in France, sitting
in a private insane asylum run by the silky plotter, Dr. Hartman. Let us hasten to say that Grace is self-committed. It
was Lefever's idea. Seems that Hartman is to receive the
snuff-box. (The Paris police know everything except how to
get the treasure back.) Naturally Hartman will not suspect
the American lady who has asked treatment for her sleep-walking.

The first night, she slips right to the Doctor's private
door and overhears him plotting. Such good luck wouldn't
happen again in sixteen years.

Next, Richard learns that the man he is after is heading
toward the sanitarium. Richard gets there first. By a
fortunate series of events that wouldn't happen again in, uh,
sixteen years, Grace happens by the door and lets Richard in.
Darling!

Darling!

Then Richard impersonates one of Hartman's henchmen, gets the snuff-box.

But he cannot escape without Grace.

He is captured.

He has only enough time to conceal the snuff-box in the hollow crown of his silk hat.

Then Hartman straps him to a table and tortures him for hours and hours by blazing a spotlight at his face.

Spying on this terrible scene, Grace's nerve fails. After the third torture session, she is wailing and crying for Richard to give up the snuff-box. (Her nerve will never again fail like this.) Meanwhile, Richard has worked himself loose in the torture-room and is frantically examining the snuff-box to understand its secret.

(By an extraordinary stroke of fortune, that wouldn't happen again for many years, the hat and snuff-box have been in the torture chamber all the time. Hartman never noticed them.)

At the last possible second, Richard solves the secret of the box: the pearls move around. There are twenty-six of them. They are keys to a complex code. Inside the box, a thin slip of paper holds the key numbers.

Enter Hartmann, cool, sneering. To me, the snuff-box geben sie hereingesein auch.

His spirit apparently shattered, Richard yields up the box and both Duvalls are released. The Paris police promptly arrest them as traitors to the French Republic.

This means that France is destroyed.

The box contained the key to the secret code in which all the secret papers were written that give vital information about French interests that is absolutely imperative the Boche shall not have information concerning although if they have the code they can decode the papers and then pouf France she is up the as you say creek hein!

Pouf! Think you Richard, he of men all, would to the enemy yield up a single secret? *Mon Dieu!* He has left a false code in the box and walked out with the true code concealed deep in his pocket, that clever one.

All is elation. "Grace,... with one cry of happiness,... flung herself into her husband's arms."

She hasn't even kissed him since they were married; it has been a most peculiar sort of honeymoon.

Covered with glory, Richard and Grace now return to America. After a modest length of time, Richard retires from the detective business in New York, turning over operations to his assistant. They buy a run-down mansion in southern Maryland and go to work as gentlemen farmers. As usual in such cases, Grace exacts Richard's promise that he will go no more adetecting.

But things keep coming up.

The next adventure is told in "The Changing Lights" (*The Cavalier*, four-part serial, January 11 through February 1, 1914; for book publication the title was changed to *The Blue Lights*.)

The son of an American millionaire is kidnapped in Paris. As usual, the French police boil helplessly. They appeal to Richard--but too late. He has just accepted the case at the request of the millionaire and is now headed to Paris by way of New Jersey. Grace believes that he has gone directly to

France and hops a liner across. On the other side, she is enlisted by Monsieur Lefever as an investigator. Lefever: "I have faith in a woman's intuition. You will find this child for me, and give your husband the surprise of his life."

This establishes the series' usual situation: Grace and Richard fly off to work independently, with Mr. Kummer performing the literary equivalent of the one step to keep them separated.

As usual, Grace has all the luck, aided by improbable coincidences and favorable stars. With remarkable dispatch, she wanders directly to the crooks' hide-out. The poor kidnapped child is there, shut up inside an enormous plaster statue.

After spending a day inside a closet, Grace is able to signal Richard. He arrives with a regiment of police and there is a fine rough and tumble. After quiet settles, Richard sums up the matter and explains all those circumstances Kummer used to expand a short story to a novel.

Back to the U.S.A. go the loving pair. So sweet, like a couple of newly weds.

To more problems.

First, the purser on a transatlantic liner vanishes with $30,000 of someone else's jewels. It is told in "The Little Fortune" (*The Cavalier*, four-part serial, August 9 through 30, 1913).

Then a bomb destroys the home of the Secretary of State in Washington. ("The Mysterious Goddess," *All-Story Cavalier*, four-part serial, April 17 through May 8, 1915; this is the only novel of the series not to appear in book form.) A suffragette was observed near the scene of the bombing. Will women stop at nothing to obtain the vote? And she has vanished, leaving only a scrap of clothing and a ten-inch doll dressed in an American flag. What can it mean?

After this case, Grace firmly insists that Richard give up detection for good. They now have a son. The farm needs work, and so time flies among the ducks and daffodils.

But peace is not for series characters. Just in time for the next novel, Grace decides that Richard needs a little mental exertion. For no wife believes that her husband can survive without constant attention and correction. In placid times, wives grow especially tense and begin worrying about their husband's mental condition. They know only too well what he is capable of if not constantly patted back into shape, like a stray curl. A safe rule is: Get His Mind Off It.

What arrives to get Richard's mind off it is "The Film of Fear" (*All-Story Weekly*, five-part serial, March 17 through April 14, 1917). Seems that the beautiful Ruth Morton, movie star from New York City, moving-picture capital of the world (which it was, then), has received letters reading:

YOUR BEAUTY HAS MADE YOU RICH AND FAMOUS. WITHOUT IT YOU COULD DO NOTHING. WITHIN THIRTY DAYS IT SHALL BE DESTROYED AND YOU WILL BE HIDEOUS.

Sealed with a skull in wax.

This message unsettles Ruth something wonderful.

Richard disguises himself, exactly like a real-true detective, and goes to Ruth's apartment. There he learns that threatening letters are appearing out of the air, dropped in

a room where the only open window faces an empty courtyard.
Near the window is a freshly painted fire escape and the paint
shows *no marks at all!*
  Replacing his disguise, Richard now goes to the movie set.
No leads. Then a defaced photograph of Ruth is delivered.
This gives her the fantabs. Richard traces the picture to the
movie president's office and, once again, a dead end.
  Now, at night, a fearful face floats frowning over Ruth's
bed, staring down into her eyes.
  She has seizures and palpitations.
  To keep her from shaking free of her bones, Richard ar-
ranges that Ruth and her mother move to other rooms. Then he
prepares a sly stratagem. He has a special strip of film pre-
pared and inserted into Ruth's new movie. And suddenly, at
the gala prevue, there flashes upon the screen a large skull
with the words

WE KNOW THE WOMAN!

  Causing a woman in the audience to rear back and faint.
Since she later evades Richard's questions, he concludes that
she is guilty. Her name is Marcia Ford and she works in the
movie president's office.
  Meanwhile ....
  Grace has intercepted a threatening telephone call for
Ruth. Attempting to tell Richard, she unwittingly reveals the
secret lodgings of Ruth and mother. Immediately, Miss Ford
appears to throw a pungent liquid into Ruth's face. Grace
trails Ford to another apartment but is attacked and choked
unconscious.
  She wakes, all tied up, to hear Miss Ford and another
woman talking. Here's what the conspiracy amounts to:

[Miss Ford:] I've gotten my revenge on that baby-faced Morton
girl. The stuck-up thing. I'll bet she won't act again in a
hurry. What right does she have to be getting a thousand a week,
when they wouldn't give me a chance at any price? I may not be
as good looking as she is, but I'm a better actress. I hate her.
I believe she told the director I wouldn't do--that's why I
didn't get the job.

  As this harangue concludes, in bursts Richard. With a
fierce sound, a terrible figure leaps at him. Before he
recognizes it as a monkey in a red silk suit, he shoots and
kills it.
  The secret is revealed. It was the monkey that delivered
the letters. It was the monkey that did not mark the paint.
It was the monkey that peered weirdly into faces. Explains
a lot.
  So now they have caught Marcia Ford with a dead monkey.
But there's no proof she did anything. Until Richard deducts
that the skull seal, used to sign the terror letters, must be
concealed in her umbrella.
  And so it is. She confesses. Since she is unbalanced,
they agree to let her go--if she will return home to Rochester
where, apparently, her affliction will not be noticed.
  And so the series closes, its final story as insubstantial
as a silken wisp. Ruth, by the way, got a facefull of ammonia
but is not hurt at all.

Such routine excitements as "The Film of Fear" were common throughout the history of *The Cavalier* and *Argosy All-Story*. No higher virtue was required of a serial than that it temporarily amuse and seduce next week's dime from the reader. Thousands of similar stories fill the magazines. They deserve neither condemnation nor memory.

From our perspective, the stories are less important than the presentation of Grace Duvall. In turn-of-the-century fiction, numbers of single women went adventuring--adventuring in the nice sense. After the marriage ceremony, they tamed down suddenly, content to wear sensible shoes and speak with authority to the Irish maid. Marriage was too serious to spend it, like small change, bustling about disguised, constantly menaced by ruffians smelling of cigars and wine. Marriage ended as much as it began.

In popular fiction, marriage was portrayed with rigid conservatism. If the magazines swallowed up the most trifling technological change and turned each of these into a series, they were excessively cautious about fiction depicting changes in social mores. Long after the ancient social cliches about women and marriage had begun to break up in practice, popular fiction remained glued to the images of the past.

Certain of these images remain familiar today: Since women are fragile and scented and dress oddly, they cannot be taken seriously. They are all emotion and whim, lacking orderly thought processes. They decorate themselves. It is true that they have an innate spirituality, permitting them to sense concealed truth. Don't even have to think about it: they just know. How cunning.

But even popular fiction, blushing red, must recognize change.

Out there in the startling world, nice women joined the suffragettes and spoke incomprehensibly about votes and government. They drove automobiles. Some smoked. Or powdered.

Surely the wraith of Mary Wollstonecraft must have grinned.

Eventually, brave editors published fiction telling of married women who did not huddle in their husbands' shadows. Not bold minxes, these, but modest, surprisingly competent women, dipping into danger without soiling their purity.

Grace Duvall is an early step along this road. Marriage did not extinguish her. Her experiences dictated the story. Modesty Blaise may consider her prim, but how refreshing Grace was to the readers of 1912.

(Continued from page 22) A fine performance. (Bob Adey)

Francis Selwyn. *Sergeant Verity and the Swell Mob*. André Deutsch, 1981.

I'm not keen on mysteries with historical settings, but Sergeant Verity is the one man I will gladly read at any time. Here in this, his fifth and latest adventure, he pits his wits against a mob of tricksters led by an old and crafty exchange broker, Sealskin Kite. There are superbly drawn pictures of a mid-victorian seaside resort and of a prison ship in all its horrifying detail. Not as bawdy as the previous books (well, you can't have everything!), it nevertheless provides first-

(Continued on page 36)

It's About Crime
By Marvin Lachman

If, for any reason, you had to restrict your purchases to one publisher, your best bet would be Perennial Library. Someone there named Hugh Van Dusen has excellent taste and has consistently not only selected quality books but also picked those not usually reprinted. For example:

1. John and Emery Bonnett's *Dead Lion* (originally 1949; $2.50). Professor Mandrake investigates the murder of an urbane but vindictive critic. Well written, with sophisticated dialogue, this represents a high degree of escape because it is a mystery puzzle that is about people very different from the kind of crime-prone individuals we might encounter in our lives and in newspapers. I look forward to reading the Bonnett's *Banner for Pegasus* (originally 1951; $2.50) from the same publisher.

2. Simon Troy's *Swift to Its Close* (originally 1969; $2.50). The puzzle and solution are okay but not as good as the setting, a British classical music festival. The characters are individuals, nicely limned by the author, who also writes as Thurman Warriner. Again, I have another Troy to look forward to as Perennial has just published the earlier *Road to Rhuine* (originally 1952; $2.95).

3. Christianna Brand's *Green for Danger* (originally 1944; $2.50). An adroit puzzle, but also a fine "period piece" which captures World War II in Britain, especially a hospital in Kent. Inspector Cockrill is a delight, and Brand does a superb job of portraying the characters' war-time nerves, which are at the breaking point.

4. Hillary Waugh's *Last Seen Wearing* (originally 1952; $2.50). One of the first and best police procedurals ever written, because it does not scatter its effect by trying to tell six cases at once. Instead, it concentrates on the efforts of Police Chief Frank Ford of Bristol, Massachusetts, to find a missing college co-ed. (Ford was apparently the forerunner of Waugh's series character, Police Chief Fred Fellows, who is featured in *The Missing Man*, another Perennial reprint [originally 1964; $2.50].) This is a simple story, but one which is told with considerable emotional impact.

Bantam has been doing a lot of old-fashioned detective

stories recently, including some by Rex Stout, Catherine Aird, E.X. Ferrars, and Carter Dickson, whose second Sir Henry Merrivale book, *The White Priory Murders* (1934), has just been published at $2.50. This book has one of Carr-Dickson's favorite ploys, murder in a setting where the absence of footprints seems impossible. He's done this before on beaches, newly brushed tennis courts, and, this time, newly-fallen snow.

My favorite spy fiction is the short stories of Michael Gilbert, and that under-rated writer has just had the second collection about his espionage team, *Mr. Calder and Mr. Behrens,* published by Harper & Row at $12.95. If not quite the equal of the first C-B collection, *Game Without Rules,* this is still a remarkably consistent collection, with two real high spots, "The Emergency Exit Affair" and "The African Tree Beavers." Gilbert's elderly agents are decent, intelligent gentlemen who are never given to the double crosses and depressions found in so many spies who have come in from the cold.

In reviewing *The Falcon and the Snowman* last year, I decried the ease with which obvious risks infiltrated our defense industry. According to *The Philby Conspiracy* (Ballantine, $2.75), the British were no better. They let people who were clearly unstable emotionally and politically into their Secret (Ha!) Intelligence (Ha!) Service. Kim Philby was the most famous. He was a communist who, as a cover, acted like a fascist. Therefore, he should have been excluded on either count. He had mental problems and drank heavily, though in those areas he couldn't compare to the two clowns, Guy Burgess and Donald Maclean, who were his fellow spies. The fourth man was Sir Anthony Blunt, a famous art historian who, until his role as spy was recently disclosed, was Keeper of the Queen's Pictures for Elizabeth II.

This non-fiction work, part of Ballantine's excellent Espionage/Intelligence Library, is better than almost any spy novel you can find. It was written by Bruce Page, David Leitch, and Phillip Knightley in the late 1960's but has been updated and includes an introduction by John Le Carré, who is *their* fourth man. Le Carré's fifteen page preface is so good that it is almost, by itself, worth the price of the book.

If you are going to read spy *novels,* you can't do much better than George Markstein, the former British crime reporter who created that strange TV series, *The Prisoner.* His *Traitor* (originally published in Britain as *Traitor for a Cause* in 1979) was reprinted last year by Ballantine for $1.95. It is an unusual combination of a sophisticated spy novel and a detective story about the series murders of Soviet defectors who have been given new identities in the U.S. Suspense is excellent; only the ending is disappointing. Just out from Balantine is *Ultimate Issue* ($2.75), Markstein's latest, a Cold War spy story set in 1961. He does a nice job of bringing together a lot of people and a lot of sub-plots, but once again that old devil ending gives him trouble. Also, this is a book in which it becomes very difficult to tell which side anyone is on. Therefore, we get such clichéd conversations of this genre as these:

"You of all people ... working for them."
"Not working for them, one of them all along."

And:

"You work for them, don't you?"
"Who's them?"
"I don't know anymore, but I can guess."

    Gregory Mcdonald has written his best mystery yet in *The Buck Passes Flynn*, a paperback original from Ballantine (at $2.25). It has a lot going for it, including the absence of Mcdonald's other series character, Fletch, whom I find to be an a moral smartass. Also, Mcdonald has given his imagination free rein, and the result is a wildly original book. Take the attention-grabbing opening sentence, for example: "From across the men's room Flynn aimed his gun at the President of the United States." The unusual plot concerns the fact that in three U.S. locations every man, woman, and child is given $100,000 anonymously. What happens tells a lot about our current values, and there is also much about our economy. Who is distributing the money proves to be an interesting mystery, though not the best part of this book.

    In *Beams Falling: The Art of Dashiell Hammett* (Bowling Green University Popular Press, Bowling Green, Ohio 43403, $13.95 cloth, $6.95 paper), Peter Wolfe has done an interesting book-length analysis of Hammett's work. In this, as in many "academic" books, the author spends an inordinate amount of time searching for literary values and the author's intent, and not enough space considering the readers for whom Hammett wrote. This is the kind of book that could be used in a college course on Hammett. There are footnotes, as required in Academe, but neither an index nor a check list of his work. The mystery fan would have appreciated those more than the footnotes, especially a complete list of the short stories.

    The short stories are handled a bit skimpily, but the novels are well handled and discussed with real insight. Still, too much is read into Hammett's words to satisfy Wolfe's theories, e.g., that Ned Beaumont was the embodiment of his creator. He may have been, but Wolfe does not convince, and he does not make his audience care that they may have been provided with some interesting information. Also, some of the language he uses is sadly inflated, e.g., words like "Englished" (a verb, God help us!) and "actionism."

    Still, Peter Wolfe has chosen some very apposite quotations from the Hammett canon to illustrate how good a writer Hammett was and how effective his terse prose was. Wolfe is especially good regarding the Continental Op, who, despite the fame of Sam Spade and Nick Charles, remains Hammett's best creation. Incidentally, what a great TV Continental Op William Conrad would have made when he was younger.

    Avon seems to have cornered the "theme" anthology market. Following their collection of Christmas mysteries late in 1981 is *The Big Apple Mysteries* (261 pages, $2.75), edited by Carol-Lynn Waugh, Martin Greenberg, and Isaac Asimov. This generous collection of New York—based mysteries has some beauties, e.g., Ellery Queen's "The Adventure of the One-Penny Black" (1934), Clayton Rawson's "From Another World" (1948), and James Yaffe's "Mom in the Spring" (1954). There is also one of those exciting, breathtaking, and unbelievable Cornell Woolrich stories, "The Phantom of the Subway" (1936). With a group of Woolrich novels due for reprint this summer, we may be in for a revival of that master's work. I can hardly wait.

    Richard Meyers' *TV Detectives* (A.S. Barnes & Co., P.O. Box

3051, La Jolla, CA 92038, 276 pp., $14.95) carries a hefty price for a trade paperback, but it is also crammed with a lot of interesting information. Meyers, who reviews TV mysteries for TAD, provides a chronological history of TV detective shows since 1947, describing the protagonists, the types of cases they solved, and the actors who appeared in the shows. There are 130 pictures, but a book of this sort could have 530 and it still wouldn't be enough.

There's nothing dry about the text, since Meyers is more than willing to express his opinion and call a turkey a turkey. Those shows he liked, he describes in a way that captures all that was good. As a result, he makes me sorry that I did not watch a few of them while they were available. Has anyone noticed how ready the television networks are to jettison their recent history? There are miles of tape and film around of shows that were infinitely better than most of the current stuff, but they are never shown. Don't they realize that they are new to current generations and they are missing a new audience?

For a book providing as much factual information as this one does, there are surprisingly few errors of omission or fact. Meyers usually gives the source when a TV detective is based on mystery novels or short stories, but he omits Roy Huggins, who created Stu Bailey before *77 Sunset Strip*. However, he traces *The Name of the Game* to a Tiffany Thayer novel that I can neither remember nor find in Hubin's *Bibliography*. Meyers is also error-prone where Howard Duff is concerned. He has Duff starring in the movie version of *Naked City*, when it was really Don Taylor. He claims that an inspector in the Charlie Chan series was named Duff in homage to Howard Duff who had played Sam Spade; he forgets that there was an Inspector Duff who appeared in at least two of Biggers' Chan novels.

This is a coffee table book you'll actually read. It's ideal in short doses. In fact, every twelve minutes I found myself wanting to stop and go to the refrigerator for a beer.

DEATH OF A MYSTERY WRITER

Harriet Adams died in New Jersey at the age of 89. Mrs. Adams, daughter of Edward Stratemeyer, continued the series regarding Nancy Drew, the Hardy Boys, Tom Swift Jr., et al that her father created. Many a mystery reader has said that she was "hooked" on mysteries while reading one of the Nancy Drew series published under the Carolyn Keene pseudonym.

W.R. Burnett died in Santa Monica at the age of 82. William Riley Burnett wrote thirty-nine novels, many of which became famous movies, including *Little Caesar*, *High Sierra*, and *The Asphalt Jungle*. He moved to Hollywood in the 1930's and became one of the best-paid script writers, specializing, as he did in his books, in gangster and war stories.

Richard Lockridge died in North Carolina at the age of 83. Though he began his career as drama critic for the *New York Sun* from 1928 to 1943, Lockridge gained fame, with his first wife, Frances, as creator of Mr. and Mrs. North. There were twenty-six North novels; the *New York Times* obit incorrectly said there were fifty. Frances Lockridge died in 1963. Richard married Hildegarde Dolson in 1965, and she began publishing mysteries herself in 1971. She died in 1981.

Reel Murders
Movie Reviews by Walter Albert

I am beginning to think that recommending films to friends should be relegated to the same, ill-advised category as counseling friends who are battling toward divorce or who want to prevent their teenagers from making the mistakes yours did.

E.T. made me feel better about children and aliens than anything since *Close Encounters,* and the newly released French import *Diva* provoked in me similar positive feelings toward opera singers, French postal employees, and fourteen-year-old Vietnamese flower children. I thought it the most exhilarating thriller in my recent memory, the most stylish, the most imaginative in its use of fairy-tale elements to grace a rather unlikely mix of operamania/record pirating/corrupt police officials/drugs and prostitution with wit, affection, and visual beauty. I also liked the references to other film directors (of which the most engaging was the Renoir sequence involving a "blind" beggar) and wallowed in the sentimental ending. The friends to whom I had recommended the film stared glumly into space when I asked them what they had thought of it. One of them muttered something about the film being too "self-conscious," while the other was more to the point: "Why, when I see only two films a year, does one of them have to be *Diva*?" Well, I will say no more except to add that I think that *Diva* may be a movie buff's delight, but too special for some people's tastes, and if you happen to see it and don't like it, don't complain to me. I'm only recommending it to myself, and I am going to see it a second time.

Although I have been seeing the new releases (*Conan, Poltergiest, Diner, The Long Good Friday* and *Star Trek II*) at a furious pace and generally enjoying them, I must report that the most disappointing film of the summer for me has been Carl Reiner's 1940s pastiche, *Dead Men Don't Wear Plaid*. I thought the opening, as Rachel Ward, looking smashing, faints on private eye Steve Martin's office stoop, was a perfect beginning to what I fully expected to be a delightful ninety minutes, but expectations have seldom been as cruelly dashed as they were for me on that unhappy Wednesday afternoon. After experiencing some momentary pleasure at the sometimes skillful blending of cuts from classic and not-so-classic forties films with the narrative, I began to feel hostility toward the tricksters who had hoked up some splendid film clips and was downright angry with Carl Reiner's outrageously bad and unfunny Nazi impersonation that closes the film. Or almost

close it. The end credits in which the familiar faces and
films from the past were identified was fun and suggested to
me that this might have been a good idea for a very short film
but was a very bad idea for a feature-length one. Both Martin
and Ward were fetching, Miklos Rosza had written a good pastiche of his own style, and the black-and-white photography
was refreshing. I think that part of my dissatisfaction with *Dead Men* was
the fact that within the last month I had seen a batch of
films noir. I saw them under the best and worst of circumstances: with a small group of film people in a University
Media Center screening room where we sat on what felt like
stone seats. I had either not seen many of the films or had
not seen them in thirty years, and for several of the other
viewers it was a first viewing of what is just a sampling from
a very rich period, 1945-1955. I am not going to review all
of the eight films in detail, but I want to list them and report on some of my impressions.

The Big Combo (1955). Director: Joseph Lewis. Screenplay:
Philip Yordan. Cinematography: John Alston. Music: David
Raksin. Featuring: Cornel Wilde, Richard Conte, Brian
Donlevy, and Jean Wallace.

Wilde, a detective investigating mobster Conte's activities, is obsessed with breaking up Conte's operation and win-
ning his mistress (Jean Wallace) for himself. Superbly
scripted, directed, and photographed, this film by a director
I had never heard of reminded me how little I know about this
period. There is a brilliant beginning as Wallace runs down
an alley with the fluidity of a trapped moth in beautifully
composed and lighted frames. One of the strongest performances
of his career is given by Brian Donlevy as a deposed mobster
chief who's now relegated to backing up Conte. He wears a
hearing-aid, and Conte, who likes to torment him by turning up
the mechanism and shouting, turns it off as Conte is gunned
down by Conte's two henchmen (Lee Van Cleef and Earl Holliman).
The guns blaze in complete silence as the shots light up the
dark and the film. The reaction of more knowledgeable members
of the audience was that this is certainly a fine film but
that Lewis's masterpiece is *Gun Crazy* (1950).

Raw Deal (1948). Director: Anthony Mann. Photography: John
Alston. Featuring: Dennis O'Keefe, Claire Trevor, Marsha
Hunt, John Ireland, and Raymond Burr.

Claire Trevor, who narrates the film in her husky, bruised
voice, helps O'Keefe escape from prison, and they head for the
Big Bad Guy (Burr), taking with them O'Keefe's sympathetic
correspondent, Marsha Hunt. The film's brutality is still
startling, especially a scene in which effete gangster Burr,
angry at a girl who has spilled liquor on him, ignites a
warming-dish and throws it in her face. The girl is off-
camera but the shock of that gesture, in which almost everything is left to the viewer's imagination, is still powerful.
O'Keefe is an actor of limited resources and Hunt is too pert
and glossy, but Trevor is very fine as the rejected girl-

friend. It's a film of multiple betrayals and is less smooth
than *The Big Combo*, but its very rawness adds to its impact.

The next five films I had seen before or found to be of
lesser interest: John Stahl's *Leave Her to Heaven* (1945), a
color treatment of predatory female Gene Tierney and fall-guy
lover Cornel Wilde; Henry Hathaway's *House on 92nd Street*
(1945), a pulpish tribute to the FBI in a semi-documentary
style which was thought at the time to be innovative; Edgar
G. Ulmer's *Ruthless* (1948), less poetic than his *Bluebeard*
(1944) but benefitting from a moody beginning in the style of
Citizen Kane and *King's Row* and an impressive performance by
Sydney Greenstreet as a Southern magnate who loses his empire
and his wife to ruthless Zachary Scott; and two Alan Ladd—
Veronica Lake pairings, the fine *Glass Key*, on which I com-
mented in my first column, and their debut performances in the
jingoistic *This Gun for Hire* (Frank Tuttle, 1942).
The last film in this short series was *Phantom Lady*, from
the novel by Cornell Woolrich. (Director: Robert Siodmak;
Photography: Woody Bredell; Cast: Franchot Tone, Ella Raines,
Alan Curtis, Thomas Gomez, and Elisha Cook, Jr.) This is a
handsomely staged but wildly improbable tale of an architect
(Curtis) who is wrongly convicted of his wife's murder and of
his Girl Friday's attempt to track down the real murderer.
Curtis is, as usual, bland, and G.F. Raines overacts (something of a feat for someone with very modest acting talents),
but Tone has some good scenes as a charmer with a flaw and
Elisha Cook's murder is well-staged. At its best, Woolrich's
world in which shadows seem to pulsate with threats and menace
is splendidly captured in this uneven film with its uneasy
blend of glibness and implicit peril. Woolrich can't be beat
for texture and atmosphere, and Siodmak and his team have
managed to get some of that on film.
Some of these films probably look better than they did
thirty years ago, and I wonder what I might think of *Diva* or
Dead Men in 2010. I will make no predictions on that, but I
suspect that *The Big Combo*, a film in which all the elements
seem to be in perfect balance, will continue to improve with
age, and I hope that the other Lewis films I may see will con-
firm my very favorable impression of this talented director.

(Continued from page 29) class entertainment.
N.B. The soft-porn series of Verity short stories that I
previously reported eventually ran through four Christmas
issues of *Men Only* from 1977 to 1980 inclusive. (Bob Adey)

Michael Hardwick. *Prisoner of the Devil*. Proteus, 1979.

Subtitled "Sherlock Holmes' Most Challenging Case," it is
the record of the maestro's investigation into the Dreyfus
Case, a real-life French affair of the eighteen-nineties.
Holmes is called in by relatives of the unfortunate Dreyfus to
discover the mysterious, and well-guarded, circumstances in
which Alfred Dreyfus, an unfortunate Jewish artillery officer,
has been convicted of treason and condemned to life imprisonment on Devil's Island.
The author does very well in capturing the essence of the
(Continued on page 49)

Mystery*File
Short Reviews by Steve Lewis

Michael L. Cook, compiler. *Monthly Murders*. Greenwood Press, 1982, 1147 + xvii pp., $49.95.

Most of this review--and it's a long one (forget about the title of this column for a while, will you?)--most of this review, as I started to say, will consist of things that displeased me about this book, and yet, surprisingly enough, much of this will have little to do with my overall opinion of it.

If you didn't already know, the subtitle will tell you exactly what this book is: "A Checklist and Chronological Listing of Fiction in the Digest Size Mystery Magazines in the United States and England."

I've already learned a lot from it, and I expect to keep learning a good deal from it in the future.

The book could be more complete, and to a considerable extent I blame only myself that it is not. (Who better should I blame?) Information concerning the contents of certain issues of some magazines like *Guilty, Trapped Detective Story Magazine* and *Suspense* is completely missing. It could have been filled in if I'd been able to clean up my study in time to locate the issues in question. I'm sorry I didn't, but, then again, I still haven't.

The majority of the listings *are* complete, however, especially (you will be glad to hear) for the magazines everybody knows about: *Ellery Queen's Mystery Magazine, The Saint Detective Magazine, Manhunt,* and so on.

However--and here start the quibbles--the listing of the magazines for which the contents are given, issue by issue, is alphabetical, *not by title but by the two-letter code that each magazine is assigned.* For example, *Ellery Queen's Mystery Magazine* is given the (logical) designation of EQ. *Mystery Book Magazine,* however, is denoted by MB, causing it to fall between *Malcolm's* (MA) and *Menace* (MC), whereas you'd certainly be more tempted to look for it between *The Mysterious Traveler Magazine* (MY) and *Mystery Monthly* (MO). What really causes problems is when *John Creasey Mystery Magazine* is listed with the C's (as CR) and not with the J's at all.

Begining on page 761 there is a *true* alphabetical listing of every magazine included here, but unless you've memorized the code labels it's still a chore to find a particular magazine's contents where you'd want to most.

Speaking of *John Creasey,* to tell the truth I'm a little

38

sorry Mike found the need to include British magazines at all,
since most of them are but reprints of the American versions,
and the contents are invariably duplicated from one to the
other. Creasey's magazine *would* be an exception to this, it
should be noted, and so would *London Mystery Magazine*. (It
would be beside the point to add that I've always found the
latter to be dull and uninteresting, wouldn't it?)

For my own part, it was nice to learn that four issues of
Manhunt on my wantlist were never published, and that I now
have only four issues left to complete my collection. The
April 1957 issue of *Alfred Hitchcock's Mystery Magazine* never
came out either, so I still need only five of those for a full
set. (I bought the first issue at the newsstand, so I always
knew the first issue was Vol. 1, No. 12.)

On the other hand, when *Homicide Detective Story Magazine*
became *Killers Mystery Story Magazine* with its second issue,
that fact is not noted with the *Homicide* listing, but it is
with *Killers,* where the contents listing is picked up with the
third issue, not the second.

(I had been told by a dealer that this magazine then became *Terror Detective Story,* but I see now from the dates and
the volume numbering of the latter that this is quite impossible. Never totally believe everything a dealer tells you.)

Unfortunately, my box of *Black Mask* pulps is buried in the
basement--well, I know exactly where it is, and it's on the
bottom--so I'm only 95% sure of this, but toward the end of
its run (circa 1951) *Black Mask* was published in the same
intermediate size between "pulp" and "digest" that *Detective
Fiction* and *New Detective Magazine* also were for a while.

Now these issues of the latter are listed, but those for
Black Mask are not. Even if I'm wrong on the above, there *was*
a one-shot attempt at reviving *Black Mask* that came out in the
early 70's, I believe--and I don't know why at all I don't
have the date handy--and that's not listed here either. It
should have been.

But arguments like this can go on forever--what should
have been included and what not? The first five issues of
Saturn Web were totally science fiction, and there's no real
reason why they should have been listed here. I have a digest-
sized issue of *Adventure* somewhere around here--well, it was
right here a minute ago--and, although it's certainly on the
borderline, it has a Bill Pronzini story in it, which says
something for it, at least, and it could have gone in too.

But let's move on. The index of stories by author is
exceedingly useful to have, and the attempt to cross-file
authors by pseudonym helps too. This list of pen-names is
hardly complete, but it's doubtful that anybody anywhere knows
who wrote exactly what, and when, for some of the more obscure
magazines.

I *was* puzzled by the reference under Lawrence Block to
"see Paul Kavanagh," since, while Jack Kavanagh has a listing,
Paul Kavanagh does not.

No attempt is made to indicate who wrote (or is writing)
the Mike Shayne novelettes by Brett Halliday, sometimes a/k/a
Davis Dresser, who, while a talanted writer, cannot still be
producing them from the grave. (I'm told that James M. Reason-
er has done a ton of them in recent years.)

Peter Reed was (usually, at least) John D. MacDonald, but
it's not noted here.

My biggest source of discontent with the author index,
however--besides the nearly incomprehensible letter coding for
the magazines, which I've neither memorized nor wholly mastered
yet--is that dates are not given for a story, but only the
volume and number for the magazine in which it appeared. "One-
Man Operation," by Carl Henry Rathjen, to pick an example entirely at random, is denoted as coming from GL 1 4, which
means not *Guilty* (nor even *Guiding Light*), but instead *The
Girl from Uncle Magazine*, Vol. 1, No. 4. What month and year?
Turn way back to the magazine listings to find out: June, 1967.

Space is always a problem in ventures such as this, but in
this case wouldn't a simple "6-67" have been tremendously more
useful? The way it is, it's certainly very difficult to get a
proper perspective on an author's career from what we see here,
with no way to know what he/she was writing when, and when it
was exactly that he/she was at his/her peak of production.

But what the hey, as they say in the barnyard. I paid
list price for this book, and I'm certainly not at all sorry
I did. Forgive the nitpicking. (It's a nasty job, but some-
body's got to do it.) All in all, it's a fantastic job. I
never expected to see a book like this in print, and here it
is.

Thanks, Mike.

(Continued from page 2) next, by the beautiful artwork of Frank
Hamilton, one of the greatest pulp fans of all. Volume one,
number one, is dated August 1982 and includes articles by Link
Hullar, Bob Sampson, Nick Carr, Will Murray, and Rex E. Ward,
plus reviews by Tom Johnson. This is all great stuff, even if,
like me, you can't bear to read the pulps themselves--reading
about them is something entirely different. Subscriptions are
$10 per year; single issues are $1.75. Mail checks to Fading
Shadows, Inc., Rt. 1, Box 169, Knox City, TX 79529.

One last item before I stagger off and try to make my
printing press do its tricks. I don't recall off hand if I've
mentioned it, but Bob and Phyllis Weinberg (15145 Oxford Dr.,
Oak Forest, IL 60452) run a bookstore-by-mail for mystery and
science fiction fans that you should know about. They are not
used-book dealers; they stock and sell new stuff that is difficult to get except through specialty stores or directly from
the publishers themselves. Write to them for a catalogue. Or,
if you prefer, a catalog.

Ooops, here's something I almost missed--Richard and Jane
Williams are booksellers specializing in crime, mystery, and
Edgar Wallace items. They issue catalogues and would like to
hear from interested collectors. They can be reached at 17
North St., Winterton, Scunthorpe, South Humberside, England.

And--of course--there's something else that I have to do
before signing off, and that's apologize for the shortness of
Steve Lewis's column in this issue, as well as the Verdicts
section. I had, in fact, already typed up fifteen pages of
reviews for this issue when several articles arrived which I
wanted very much to get in this time around. The only way to
do it was to cut back Verdicts drastically and restrict
Mystery*File to a single (albeit long) review. I hope the
review lovers among you--not to mention those whose reviews
were bumped--will forgive me; I assure you all that the
reviews will be back in force once this issue and the index
issue are out of the way.

Verdicts
More Reviews

Max Collins. *Nolan #5: Hard Cash*. Pinnacle, 1982, 180 pp.,
   $1.95.

Professional criminal Nolan is going straight now as co-
owner and manager of a seafood restaurant "on the banks of the
Iowa River," but his criminal past confronts him in the person
of George Rigby, president of a local bank that Nolan had held
up a couple of years earlier. Rigby is being eased out of his
executive position and, knowing that his unfortunate habit of
using bank funds for his own purpose will be disclosed in the
next audit, wants Nolan to bring off a hit that will enable
Rigby to restore the missing funds and support him and his
ambitious mistress in his new life. His lever with the unwilling Nolan is a series of compromising photographs, and
Nolan and Jon, Nolan's young comic collector and artist sidekick, agree to co-operate and begin to set up the operation for
Christmas Eve.
   Collins' second plot line also concerns an incident in
Nolan's past, with murderous Sam Comfort and his surviving son,
Terry, out to avenge their treatment by Nolan and his friends
in an earlier drama of betrayal and revenge. The two plots--
the bank job and the Comforts' vengeance--coincide at the
bloody climax of a sordid, improbable, and entertaining web of
deceit and coincidence.
   Collins returns here to the competent form of the first two
Nolan novels, and my only complaint concerns the padded exposi-
tion (for the convenience of readers unfamiliar with the earlier
novels) and the coincidental deliverance of Nolan and Breen in
the climax and denouement. Everyone's plans go awry in this
novel, and Nolan is as much a victim as the other characters,
although he is luckier than any of his antagonists. The fates
do conspire to do in the "truly" wicked, but they also do in
one of Nolan's confederates and spare Nolan himself a couple of
turns of the wheel that seem intended only to leave the way
open for the next book in the series. Sidekick Jon is still an
appealing character, made all the more so by his reluctance to
continue his life of crime. Nolan has been compared to Richard
Stark's Parker, but the Collins' series lacks the bitter edge
and power of the Stark novels, although this is a good suspense
melodrama in a minor key. (Walter Albert)

Donald Zochert. *Another Weeping Woman*. Holt, Rinehart and
    Winston, 1980.

A young woman camper is apparently mauled and killed by a
bear. The autopsy establishes that she also had a bullet in
her head and that she was dead before either the bullet or the
bear got her. A good start, and then it's downhill all the
way. The main problem with this book is the style: "The thing
I'll remember most is the car horn. The sound of that car
horn just after dawn--filling the little valley with its
wounded cry, echoing off those cliffs and rising up the cirque
in that cold September air to the face of the Grasshopper itself." This is the opening paragraph, and the portentous,
tense tone is maintained for 262 pages. "The house had been
taken over by darkness. The wind cried in through the shattered windows, the wind and the darkness and the night rasping
past the teeth of glass that grinned in the wooden frames."
This is a desperate, adjective-laden, overwritten novel, and
if the angst-ridden symphonies of Mahler or a hysterical guitar
savagely resounding in a shadowy, empty hall crouching in a
hungry night are your sound, you'll have a grand time. I'll
have a soda with a twist of lime, thank you, Archie.
    Post-scriptum. In this year of our Lord, 1982, it is still
possible to find a novel that features a "Mr. Big." (Walter
Albert)

Sheila Radley. *A Talent for Destruction*. Constable, 1982,
    160 pp.

Organizationally, Sheila Radley's third Douglas Quantrill
mystery is a bit reminiscent of Dick Francis' latest novel,
Twice Shy, in that Radley also breaks her story at its center.
"Part 1--this winter" recounts the efforts of Chief Inspector
Quantrill to solve the mystery of a skeleton found in Parsons'
Close; because of the refusal of any suspect to talk, he fails,
though he comes close. "Part 2--last summer" begins all over
again, shifting to the perspective of Gillian Ainger, wife of
the rector at Breckhan Market, Quantrill's manor; in this section, a long flashback, Radley lays out, cooly, deliberately,
fully, the true events leading up to the murder ... and again
stops short of full explanation. "Part 3--this spring" resumes
Quantrill's point of view and the "present" time, leading to
the final revelation. The real stinger comes in "Part 4--New
Hampshire, last fall"; set in another country, this section in-
cites regret that the wench is *not* dead.
    In several ways, Radley's experiment is even more success-
ful than Francis'; she adds handily to her readers' growing
grasp of Douglas Quantrill's complex and sometimes prickly personality, and she brings Gillian Ainger, her husband Robin,
their friend Alec Reynolds, and Australian student Janey Rolph
to vivid, effective life. Of the cast of major characters,
Gillian is perhaps the most appealing, but all are interesting
people, all, alas, capable of reminding us at least a little,
perhaps, of ourselves. Therein lies the book's considerable
power.
    As is customary in the Quantrill stories (and in multitudes
of other cop tales), the main subplot in *A Talent for Destruction*

has to do with Quantrill's family. This time out, his son,
Peter, is in trouble with the police for "several hundred
pounds' worth of damage to the church hall, apparently sus-
tained when the youth club got out of hand." The situation is
a great worry to the Detective Chief Inspector (he loves his
children, but, as with his wife, he has difficulty making his
feelings known), and it is, of course, also an embarrassment;
he hates the idea of his colleagues knowing that Peter is even
a bit out of hand. Radley never oversimplifies nor sensation-
alizes these problems, and they serve her well. Also briefly
on the scene is another regular in the Quantrill series, Martin
Tait, recently promoted and shifted to a new territory. He and
Quantrill still need and irritate one another, and their scenes
together are very well done.

In *A Talent for Destruction*, as in *The Chief Inspector's
Daughter* (1981) and *Death and the Maiden* (1978; U.S. title
Death in the Morning, 1979), Radley once again explores facets
of women's roles in contemporary society. She does not preach
but fully integrates speculation, commentary, and action, and
these explorations add a good deal of thought and value to the
novels. Radley is good; she's getting better all the time, and
A Talent for Destruction is ample proof. (Jane S. Bakerman)

Ruth Rendell. *Master of the Moor*. Hutchinson, 1982, 219 pp.

Master of the Moor comes complete with a map of Vagmoor,
its haunting, gripping setting. That's a nice, old-fashioned
touch, but it's the only thing old-fashioned about the novel,
which is a modern psychological thriller whose protagonist,
Stephen Whalby, matches the moor which so fascinates him. The
action begins when Stephen finds the body of a murdered young
woman on the moor he has come to think of as his own territory,
and the outer action depicts Stephen's confrontation with the
police who suspect him of this and of a second killing and por-
trays his forced confrontation with the reality behind his difficult and unusual marriage.

The inner action, however, is just as important. For his
entire lifetime, Stephen has coped with problems of itentity.
Privately, Stephen traces his heritage to Alfred Osborn Tace,
author of a series of novels about Vagmoor which have lately
been given new fame via a television series, for Stephen believes himself to be the son of Tace's illegitimate daughter.
He reenforces his Tace heritage by writing a series of nature
articles (as "Voice of Vagmoor") for the local paper and by
scorning his mother's family. The fact that Brenda, his mother,
had abandoned him and his grim, taciturn, depressive father
early in Stephen's childhood exacerbates his confusion of
identity--through her come both his greatest pride and his
greatest shame. Also because of Brenda's desertion, the boy
Stephen has been pulled between two strong, destructive forces,
his father and his maternal grandmother, Helena Naulls; his
responses toward both are loaded with hatred as well as a kind
of love, but he remains uneasily loyal to both relatives into
his manhood. Duty and fantasy are his mainstays; in the long
run, both fail him.

In many ways, Stephen never grows up. His marriage to Lyn
as well as his relationships with father and grandmother are
ample evidence of that. Also, instead of true development, he

substitutes an eerie ability to identify very strongly with others: the writer, Tace; his personal image of the killer (whom he calls Rip); and a boyhood companion, his cousin Peter Naulls. But most important, he identifies with Vagmoor, its brooding landscape an excellent symbol for the mindscape of Stephen's character. On Vagmoor, which, he believes, he knows better than any other living soul, Stephen feels like a king, master of the moor, its tricky terrain, its hills (foins), abandoned mineshafts (soughs), twisty trails (crinkle-crankle paths)--and of the Foinmen, huge, erect stones, reminiscent of Stonehenge and of ancient ceremony.

Thus Stephen hangs, swinging between the ancient and the modern past and the troublesome present, until the murder on the moor and his wife's decision to live freely and in the present moment precipitate Stephen Whalby's final crisis. With Stephen, as with the earlier complex, difficult protagonists of her psychological suspense novels, Rendell is dispassionate. Readers will understand Stephen, feel compassion for him, perhaps even empathy; but they will never sentimentalize him; his creator won't allow it. Wise she is not to do so. It is this sure touch which lifts *Master of the Moor* to excellence. Fans of Ruth Rendell have come to expect that; they will not be disappointed. (Jane S. Bakerman)

Tony Hillerman. *The Dark Wind*. Harper & Row, 1982.

Jim Chee, Tony Hillerman's second Navajo protagonist, returns to action in *The Dark Wind*. Now assigned to the Tuba City subagency of the Navajo Tribal Police, Chee is slowly working his way toward an effective relationship with his superior, Captain Largo. At one point, he ponders:

> The way the Navajos calculate kinship, the captain was a relative through clan linkage. Chee's crucial "born to" clan was the Slow Talking Dinee of his mother, but his "born for" clan--the clan of his father--was the Bitter Water People. Largo was born to the Standing Rock Dinee, but was "born for" the Red Forehead Dinee, which was also the secondary "born for" clan of Chee's father. That made kensmen. Distant Kinsmen, true enough, but kinsmen in a culture that made family of first importance and responsibility to relatives the highest value. Chee ... thought about kinship. But he was remembering how a paternal uncle had once cheated him on a used-refrigerator sale, and that the worst whipping he'd ever taken in the Two Gray Hills Boarding School was from a maternal cousin.

This quotation illustrates a number of Hillerman's strengths-- exploration of Navajo culture, examination of intradepartmental pressures (which couple with interdepartmental power plays), and the steady development of Jim Chee's characterization, particularly his habit of polishing his professional savvy.

Chee's first major case since his transfer from Crownpoint involves murder, a plane crash, the repeated sabotage of Windmill Number 6 (situated on land now being occupied by Hopis in the aftermath of the eviction of a number of Navajos), and drug running, as well as Native American ritual and belief--Chee has to penetrate a Hopi ceremony in order to solve his case. His investigation also involves bucking various law enforcement

power structures, and Hillerman capitalizes particularly well
the characterization of a very unsavory officer who provides
good contrast with Chee. Another sound character is Deputy
Sheriff Albert "Cowboy" Dashee, and the relationship between
the Hopi Cowboy and the Navajo Chee dramatizes the delicate
cultural balance which lies close to the center of Hillerman's
plots.
    In *The People of Darkness*, Jim Chee's first case, we
learned a good deal about Chee's personal life. Material of
that sort is disappointingly missing from *The Dark Wind*, but
that loss is the only disappointment. Hillerman has done a
good job, and *The Dark Wind* will not only satisfy in itself but
will also whet readers' appetites for more. (Jane S. Bakerman)

Emma Lathen. *Green Grow the Dollars*. Simon and Schuster,
    1982, 216 pp.

    After a slightly disappointing showing in *Going for the
Gold*, Emma Lathen (Mary Jane Latsis and Martha Henissart) and
their protagonist, banker John Putnam Thatcher, are back in
stride. As usual, the crux of the plot is a matter of invest-
ment and finance which involves the Sloan Guaranty Trust, the
Wall Street bank of which Thatcher is Senior Vice President.
The financial contenders this time are the Vandam Nursery &
Seed Company (recently acquired by Standard Foods, a major
Sloan client) and Wisconsin Seedsmen, rivals in the plant
development, seed-and-bulb sales industry.
    Both firms lay claim to a new tomato, called variously
Numero Uno and the VR-117, depending on the promotional inten-
sity of the firms who maintain they developed it and who intend
to promote it for all it's worth. It will be worth quite a
lot, for the new breed of tomato is a "genetic miracle" which
"bears like a tiger for a full six months in most places."
There's a very great deal at stake here for Wisconsin Seedsmen,
Vandams, and for the Institute of Plant Research, an independent firm which does much of Vandams' plant development and
which held the contract for *Numero Uno*, for not only are huge
profits involved, but also the sterling reputations of both
Vandams and the Institure as well as the potentially bright
future of the budding Wisconsin Seedsmen. When a Seedsmen
employee is murdered, however, even these enormous stakes
escalate, and Thatcher is once again set upon the trail of a
killer.
    As is always true in the best of Lathen, minor characters
are fascinating, and especially intriguing is Mrs. Mary Lara-
bee, present to collect the award for her home-garden-developed
Firecracker at the annual banquet of the American Sweet Pea
Society. But Mary Larrabee proves to be more than her spon-
sors, Vandams, bargain for and stays to sow the seeds of a
promising career making commercials, all in aid of sending her
kids to college. It is also Mary who gets Thatcher involved
in a pre-dawn trip to the Chicago wholesale produce market, one
of Lathen's best-realized scenes ever--Edna Ferber did it earlier, true, but good as she was, she didn't do it any better.
    A garden variety murder mystery whose first chapter is
titled "Prepare Plot Thoroughly" and whose further chapter
titles are equally funny and appropriate ("Attracts Pests" and
"Send Out Runners," for instance) can hardly miss, and *Green*
(Continued on page 18)

The Documents
In the Case
Letters

From Bob Sampson, 609 Holmes Ave. NE, Huntsville, AL 35801:
More on Charles W. Tyler. I finally found something about
him. Not very flipping much, but something concrete. All
that nicely detailed information given in "Pirates in Candy-
land" is wrong. That was not the Charles W. Tyler. According
to a profile in the 7/20/29 *Detective Story Magazine* (just
secured), Tyler was born in North Hinsdale, New Hampshire. No
date given. Was a railroad fireman, draftsman, and steamfit-
ter, among other professions. Spent a lot of time traveling,
was married, and, in 1929, lived in California. That's the
total of facts gathered from a 2-page, 4-column article. But
at least I can get rid of that other information now. I do
hope that somebody--Bleiler or other informed people--can come
up with more concrete data. It would be nice to have born/
died dates, if nothing else.

From Marvin Lachman, 34 Yorkshire Dr., Suffern, NY 10901:
I was surprised to find a six-page article on Carter Dickson's *The Peacock Feather Murders* since, by coincidence, I had
just finished reading that book only five days before my copy
of TMF arrived in the mail. Therefore, though I, personally,
was equipped with close rememberance of the plot details of
that book, I wonder how many other readers of TMF would be.
Anyone who has never read it would, of course, be well advised
not to read Bleiler's article. Anyone who had not read it
recently would not remember many of the precise details he
uses to make his points. Therefore, since TMF's main purpose
is not to instruct fledgling mystery novelists, I wonder how
useful it was to publish an article of six pages in length
that most readers will either skip or pass over quickly.
I read it slowly and carefully for several reasons.
Firstly, the book was still in my mind. Secondly, I have a
great deal of respect for E.F. Bleiler as one of the best
editors in the business. After reading his article, I have
even more respect for him since he has done a masterful job
of analyzing the plot and motivation of this book. He is
right about the weaknesses he found in the book on his re-
reading. On only two points in his analysis would I question
him, namely:
1. He claims that Carr misleads the reader by stating (as
Carr) that two revolver shots had been fired in the room. It

seems clear to me from my reading of the section in question that it was to the mind of Pollard, the policeman watching the murder room, that it appeared that two shots had been fired in the room.

2. He claims that throwing in cricket is done underhand. I believe that throwing (or bowling, as it is called) is overhand, though with a straight arm motion, unlike our overhand throwing in the U.S.

My question is why re-read a book, when there are so many books unread? Further, why take so much time to tear it apart? Sure, *Peacock* is not Carr-Dickson at his best. It's a pretty good puzzle that demands a good bit of suspension of disbelief. Yet, it is entertaining. In fact, it is almost always fun to see Carr ring another variation of the locked room theme. Was any real purpose served, Mr. Bleiler, in taking the book apart so thoroughly? [*I certainly think there was, but I'll leave it to Ev to answer if he so chooses.*]

I can't quite agree with Greg Goode regarding Bob Reiss's *Summer Fires*. Having spent the first 23 years of my life in the South Bronx area known as Fort Apache, I don't find it too good a subject for fiction. More importantly, I thought *Summer Fires* was totally unbelievable, from its hero, who lives there when he doesn't have to, to the hero's convenient next door romance. Most unbelievable of all was the reason behind the titular fires. I found the book to be a gimmicky working over of yesterday's headlines, not well-thought-out entertainment or a moving social statement.

From Jeff Banks, Box 13007 SFA Sta., Nacogdoches, TX 75962: I wish you would copy Jeff Meyerson and shift to quarterly publication. I think $12 per year for subs would still be just about right. If you got super-energetic meanwhile, you could always issue an Extra--does that idea strike a responsive chord in the old newshound? [*Ouch. Sorry to have been so late in getting the last issue out, but, as I'll explain in "Mysteriously Speaking ...", I had problems.*]

Count my vote on the side of those who like the heavy coverage on movies. Living in a small-town cultural backwater, I find it very useful to be made aware of what the local cinema (s?) may not be offering.

I continue to be delighted with Van Tilburg's "Dossier" series; am delighted that he has agreed to cover the paperback spies as well. You certainly don't need my chart articles while his series is going on! [*So that's your excuse for not writing anything lately, is it?*]

More pulp articles PLEASE! [*Always happy to oblige; see Bob's latest in this issue.*] I, and many of your other older readers, love the pulps. Now that we can't read them anymore --at least nobody seems to be manufacturing any more of them, excepting the foreshortened single *Black Mask* and 4-issue *Weird Tales* of the seventies--we love to read about them. More pulp articles PLEASE! Perhaps Bob Sampson could do you something on the various polite pulp detectives who preceded the Hardboiled ones.

Bleiler's Carr critique was a beauty, just the kind of in-depth study of a book that is only to be found in a fanzine. [*Are you listening, Marv?*] See if you can get more of those, too!

I continue to like the columns and regular departments--
except the letters. And I find I'm writing just the kind of
letter I like least, so I'll stop. However, let me say first
that I think hardworking editors like yourself probably need
letters like this (that mostly tell you what a good job you're
doing--AND YOU CERTAINLY ARE!) but they don't necessarily have
to publish them.
Keep up the beautiful work. [*Thanks. I needed that.*]

From Charles Shibuk, 2084 Bronx Park East, Bronx, NY 10462:
Marv Lachman's reference to the Soviet author Marietta S.
Shaginyan in his latest coulmn leaves me with a microscopic
nit to pick.
I didn't notice the obituary Marv cited, but this *New York
Times* section has, on occasion, been guilty of publishing mis-
information instead of fact.
The correct title of Miss Shaginyan's second book is *Miss*
(not Mess) *Mend, or the Yankees in Petrograd.*
Or was this error really another whimsical Townsend typo?
[*At long last I am delighted to be able to say* mea *not* culpa;
*it's Mess in Marv's original MS. Which does not, of course,
absolve me of responsibility, which must ultimately rest on
the editor's desk.*]
My sources claim that Miss Shaginyan's two mystery novels
were written under the pseudonym "Jim (not Jimmy) Dollar."
Cinemaddicts might note the 1926 silent Soviet film version of *Miss Mend* which was recently reported to be of considerable merit.

From Ev Bleiler, somewhere in Darkest New Jersey:
As I type this, I am thinking both sadly and angrily about
the dispersal of the Goldstone and Hubin collections, the
former not at just scalper prices, but Jivaro prices. What a
shame that collections that have taken decades to build up,
and are almost unique, and really should be national treasures,
have to be scattered about so that no one can have access to
them. In this, I am not blaming Al Hubin in the slightest,
for I can understand his point of view and I know that he
tried to sell the collection as something to be preserved. I
am blaming the incredible shortsightedness of our major lib-
raries, which were unwilling to buy either collection. It is
not wholly a matter of money, for I am sure that if another
Shakespeare first folio should come onto the market for
$100,000 there would be dozens of libraries competing to buy
it. Yet I gather that either of these detective story collections could have been bought for this price, or less.
Well, I suppose that twenty years from now the situation
will be different.

From Art Scott, 2833 Kennedy St., Livermore, CA 94550:
This is Art, assuming the unaccustomed role of pitchman on
behalf of Bouchercon. Free publicity is what we're after, and
I assume TMF will be delighted to provide same. I'm enclosing
a few copies of our initial flyer, with the vital information
on when, where, what, and how much included therein. I assume
you'll find a prominent place in the next issue to plug the

great event. Or maybe better, if you have a spare page to
fill, you could cut the flyer just below Don Herron's address,
shrink it a bit, and run the whole flyer as is. Whatever
suits you. [*See the back cover of this issue. Art's letter
and the flyer arrived after I had 6:3 all typed up, so this is
the first chance I've had to mention it. I hope the lateness
does not keep anyone from attending.*]

From David F. Wilkerson, Rt. 1, Box 5, Days Creek, OR 97425:
    I wrote to you some time ago about a new series done in
North Africa. The book is *The Leo Conversion* by David Smith
(Dodd, Mead, 1980). The main characters or detectives are
James Stevens and Mallan Mohamed Murtala Muntaka. The book
is, I think, the first in a series about the two detectives.
I think you would enjoy it. [*Thanks for the tip.*]

From Myrtis Broset, 204 S. Spalding St., Spring Valley, IL:
    Richard Lockridge passed away on June 19th at the age of
eighty-three.
    How I loved the Mr. and Mrs. North mysteries written by
Lockridge and his wife, Frances. After her death, Lockridge
went on with the Inspector Heimrich stories, followed by his
police procedural books, which were not as popular as the
earlier books, but which still made for good reading.
    How sad--another writer of our treasured mysteries has
left us.

From Becky Reineke, 1648 Zarthan Ave. S., Minneapolis, MN:
    All the discussion on format, printing technique, etc. for
reprinting TMF Volume One was interesting but for myself unnecessary. I have complete faith in you, Guy! [*Which is more
than I have in myself.*] I'm sure you'll do your usual mar-
velous job. [*No, Bill Crider and John Nieminski, I'm not making all this up.*] Now whether or not it will sell is another
matter. I think it will; $20, as a maximum, is not an exor-
bitant amount, and I would be willing to purchase the first
seven issues of TMF at that price. As you pointed out, their
reference value is severely limited if they are unobtainable.
    My run of TMF starts with Volume Four. At first I didn't
consider getting back issues because I scarcely have time to
read current ones (evidenced by this late a letter). The key
word here is "read." "Reading" and "referencing" are two different matters. The Brownstone reissues would be an excellent
addition to my, or any Johnny-come-lately's, reference shelf.
Let's keep future generations of mystery lovers in mind, huh?
    Thanks for calling attention to *Mystery News*. The sample
issue I sent for is chock full of new releases--a very handy
guide for current titles.
    I was surprised to see so much of 6:2 devoted to the
movies. Locally we've had some Hitchcock films on late TV,
most notably *The Thirty-Nine Steps* and *The Lady Vanishes*. I
even managed to catch, starting at 2:45 a.m., another Van Dine
oldie, *The Kennel Murder Case*. In this 1933 film, Vance,
again played by William Powell, solves a locked room murder.
It was worth every yawn the next day, although I've decided
these precious late movies are by themselves worth the invest-
ment in a video recorder. Leaving the home and actually

laying out money, I thought the latest Christie, *Evil Under the Sun*, was well done, and Levin's *Deathtrap* absolutely un-nerving. Look forward to comments on these two by Albert, or whomever contributes to the other column.

Guy--you must have failing eyesight. (This letter is a test--only a test....) I have had some letters from Bob Adey, and I beg to disagree. Bob's handwriting is not the disaster you proclaim. In two letters there was only one word I could-n't decipher. Perhaps he was merely being courteous, and therefore neater, with me? [*Nonsense; you simply have a gift for reading illegible handwriting. Someday I may put your gift to the supreme test by letting you work on a sample of my handwriting.*]

Curious, huh? I started the letter exchange. A puzzle freak from way back, I simply had to have Bob's *Locked Rooms* book. Since it was unavailable here in the U.S., I went directly to the source. And, bless him, he had some copies yet remaining!

From Linda Toole, 40 Hermitage Rd., Rochester, NY 14617:

Thanks for the confession. I would appreciate it if future calls were at some time other than 2 a.m. Monday morn-ing!

Here's my check for $1 for the tape-copying waiting list. My thanks in advance. I've exhausted Steve Lewis's supply of Nero Wolfe tapes.

Hope you also have me down for the facsimile of TMF Vol. 1.

You probably have plenty of work lined up, but may I sug-gest a Wolfe concordance? With more than 700 members in the Wolfe Pack and many more fans outside of the Pack, it would probably sell quite well--especially if it could be done for $20 or less. [*As a matter of fact, I have been plugging away at such a work for more than a year now. The going is pain-fully slow, as I am searching every story for clues, taking notes so extensively that the manufacturers of index cards must have declared record dividends this year, and it will be several more years before the study will finally be completed. I'm going to do it right, this time. Not the slap-dash job I did on "The Nero Wolfe Saga," and not the God-awfully bad (and inaccurate) job that Baring-Gould did in* Nero Wolfe of West Thirty-Fifth Street. *I know, I know--Baring-Gould died before the book was finished, but that doesn't excuse his grosser offenses, such as making up material which contradicts things that Wolfe's creator wrote. There are some things that Just Are Not Done.*]

(Continued from page 36) the illustrious pair, and, apart from a tacky section in the middle, the plot advances with reason-able speed and logic. The Holmes mannerisms sometimes seem lacking, but the dialogue (albeit without the instant deduc-tions) rings true. I don't know the Dreyfus details well enough to be able to say whether the eventual explanation and the Holmes/Watson activities would fit, but the grafting on has resulted in a quite healthy hybrid.

Surely one of the leaders in the current Holmes pastiche stakes. (Bob Adey)

BOUCHERCON
BY-THE-BAY

""""""""""""""""""

Robert B. Parker
GUEST OF HONOR

in San Francisco October 8-9-10, 1982

Bouchercon, the annual gathering of mystery fans and writers, goes to San Francisco for its thirteenth year of celebrating crime & punishment. San Francisco, the city where Dashiell Hammett quit the Pinkerton Agency in order to write his tales of hard-boiled detection, the city where Sam Spade sleuthed in the night-fog. Across the Bay, Anthony Boucher, after whom Bouchercon is named, wrote his classical puzzle mysteries & was a major force in developing detective fiction criticism. Bouchercon By-the-Bay will feature three days of panels covering many aspects of crime writing, from Conan Doyle's Sherlock Holmes to Robert B. Parker's Spenser. It will present a major program of mystery films, the largest dealers room offering rare & out-of-print mysteries ever seen at a crime convention, as well as the usual party rooms, signing sessions, & banquet.

Bouchercon By-the-Bay convenes at the Jack Tar Hotel, Van Ness & Geary. Single rooms are $68 per day, doubles $78; rebates will be given for those staying at the Jack Tar; also, we offer a doubling up service for singles who wish to rent a double room, based on sex, smoking or non-smoking, classical or hard-boiled....

Admission to all three days of the convention is $25 until August 15th & $30 thereafter; admission is $10 per day at the door; supporting memberships are $10, & may be used toward admission.

- -

BOUCHERCON BY-THE-BAY

Don Herron, Chairman 537 Jones St. #9207 San Francisco, Ca. 94102

_____ Please send _____ membership(s) at $25 ea. ($30 after August 15th)
_____ Please send _____ supporting membership(s) at $10 ea.

Make check or money order payable to Bouchercon By-the-Bay.

NAME _____

ADDRESS _____ PHONE _____

CITY _____ STATE _____ ZIP _____

Advertising rates for the program book
and reservations for the dealers room
available on request; enclose SASE.

www.ingramcontent.com/pod-product-compliance
Lightning Source LLC
Chambersburg PA
CBHW050906120626
46554CB00003B/1050